W9-CON-454

# THINGS WE LOST IN THE FIRE

STORIES

---

Mariana Enriquez

TRANSLATED BY MEGAN McDOWELL

HOGARTH
London / New York

This is a work of fiction. Names, characters, places, and incidents either are the product of the author's imagination or are used fictitiously. Any resemblance to actual persons, living or dead, events, or locales is entirely coincidental.



Published in the United States by Hogarth, an imprint of
the Crown Publishing Group, a division of Penguin Random House LLC,
New York.
hogarthbooks.com

HOGARTH is a trademark of the Random House Group Limited,
and the H colophon is a trademark of Random House LLC.

Originally published in Spanish in Spain as *Las cosas que perdimos en el fuego* by Editorial Anagrama, S. A., Barcelona, in 2016. Copyright © 2016 by Marianna Enriquez.

Library of Congress Cataloging-in-Publication Data is available upon request.

ISBN 978-0-451-49511-2
Ebook ISBN 978-0-451-49513-6

Printed in the United States of America

*Book design by Andrea Lau*
*Jacket design by Christopher Brand*
*Jacket illustration by Micah Lidberg*

10 9 8 7 6 5 4 3 2 1

First United States Edition

# THINGS WE LOST IN THE FIRE

## CONTENTS

# THINGS WE LOST IN THE FIRE

# The Dirty Kid

My family thinks I'm crazy, and all because I choose to live in our old family home in Constitución, in the house that once belonged to my paternal grandparents. It's an imposing stone building on Calle Virreyes, with iron doors painted green, art deco details, and old mosaics on a floor so worn out that if I ever got the urge to wax it I could open up a roller rink. But I was always in love with this house. I remember when I was little and my family rented it out to a law firm and I got so upset; I missed those rooms with their tall windows, and the walled patio that was like a secret garden. I hated not being able to just go in anytime I wanted. I never really missed my grandfather, a silent man who hardly ever smiled and never played—I didn't cry when he died. I cried a lot, though, when after he died we lost the house for several years.

After the law firm a team of dentists moved in, and then the house was rented to a travel magazine that folded in less than two years. The house was beautiful and comfortable and in remarkably good condition considering how old it was, but by then no one, or very few people, wanted to settle in that neighborhood. The travel magazine went for it only because the rent was very low. But not even that could save them from promptly going bankrupt, and it certainly didn't help that their offices were robbed: all their computers were stolen, plus a microwave oven and even a heavy photocopier.

The Constitución station is where trains coming from the south of the country enter the city. In the nineteenth century, the port's aristocracy had lived in Constitución; that's why houses like my family's exist, and there are plenty of others that have been converted into hotels or old folks' homes, or are crumbling to the ground on the other side of the station, in Barracas. In 1887, the aristocratic families fled to the northern part of the city to escape the yellow fever. Few of them came back, almost none. Over the years, families of rich businessmen like my grandfather were able to buy those stone houses with their gargoyles and bronze door knockers. But the neighborhood was marked by that flight, the abandonment, the condition of being unwanted.

And it's only getting worse.

But if you know how to move around the neighborhood, if you understand its dynamics, its schedules, it isn't dangerous. Or it's less dangerous. I know that on Friday nights, if I go down to Plaza Garay I might end up caught in a fight between several possible adversaries: the mini-narcos from Calle Ceballos who defend their territory from invaders and chase down the countless people who owe them money; the brain-dead addicts who get offended at anything and react by lashing out with broken bottles; the drunk and tired transvestites who have their own patches of pavement to defend. I also know that if I walk home along the avenue I'm more exposed to muggers than if I take Solís, even though the avenue is well lit and Solís is dark; most of the few streetlights it has are broken. You have to know the neighborhood to learn these strategies. I've been robbed twice on the avenue, both times by kids who ran past and grabbed my bag and pushed me to the ground. The first time, I filed a police report; by the second I knew it was pointless. The police let teenage muggers rob on the avenue as far as the highway bridge—three free blocks—in exchange for favors. There are certain tricks to being able to move easily in this neighborhood and I've mastered them perfectly, though sure, something unexpected can always happen. It's a question of not being afraid, of making a few necessary friends, saying hi to the neighbors even if they're criminals—especially if they're criminals—of walking with your head high, paying attention.

I like the neighborhood. No one understands why, but I do: it makes me feel sharp and audacious, on my toes. There aren't many places like Constitución left in the city; except for the slums on its outskirts, the rest of the city is richer and friendlier—huge and intense but easy to live in. Constitución isn't easy, and it's beautiful: all those once-luxurious alcoves, like abandoned temples now occupied by unbelievers who don't even know that inside those walls hymns to old gods once rang out.

There are also a lot of people who live on the street. Not as many as in Plaza Congreso, two kilometers from my front door—over there it's a regular encampment, right in front of the government buildings, scrupulously ignored but also so visible that every night squads of volunteers come to hand out food, check the children's health, distribute blankets in winter and fresh water in summer. The homeless in Constitución are more neglected, and help rarely reaches them. Across from my house is a corner with a shuttered convenience store, whose doors and windows are bricked up to keep occupiers out; a young woman lives with her son on the sidewalk in front of it. She's pregnant, maybe a few months along, although you never know with the junkie mothers in the neighborhood because they're so thin. The son must be around five years old. He doesn't go to school and he spends his days on the subway, begging for money in exchange for prayer cards of Saint Expeditus. I know because I've seen him at night, on the train, on my way home from the city center. He has a disturbing method: after offering the prayer cards to the passengers, he obliges them to shake hands, a brief and very grimy squeeze. The passengers have to contain their pity and disgust: the kid is very dirty and he stinks. Anyway, I never saw anyone compassionate enough to take him out of the subway, bring him home, give him a bath, call social services. People shake his hand, buy his prayer cards. His forehead is always wrinkled into a frown, and when he talks, his voice is shot; he tends to have a cold, and sometimes he smokes with other kids from the subway or around Constitución.

One night, we walked together from the subway station to my house. He didn't talk to me, but we kept each other company. I asked him some dumb questions, his age, his name; he didn't answer. He wasn't a sweet or innocent child. When I reached the door of my house, though, he said good-bye.

"Bye, neighbor," he said.

"Bye, neighbor," I replied.

THE DIRTY KID AND HIS MOTHER sleep on three mattresses so worn out that, piled up, they're the same height as a normal bed. The mother keeps what little clothing she has in several black garbage bags, and she has a backpack full of other things; I couldn't say what they are. She doesn't move from the corner; she stays there and begs for money in a gloomy and monotonous voice. I don't like the mother. Not just because she's irresponsible, or because she smokes crack and the ash burns her pregnant belly, or because I never once saw her treat her son, the dirty kid, with kindness. There's something else I don't like. I told my friend Lala while she was cutting my hair in her house one Monday, a holiday. Lala is a hairdresser, but she hasn't worked in a salon for a long time; she doesn't like to have bosses, she says. She earns more money and is more at ease in her apartment. As a salon, Lala's place has a few issues. The hot water, for example, only flows sporadically because the heater is busted, and sometimes, when she's washing my hair after dyeing it, I get a shock of cold water over my head that makes me cry out. Then she rolls her eyes and explains that all the plumbers cheat her, they charge her too much, they never come back. I believe her.

"Girl, that woman is a monster," she yells as she burns my scalp with her ancient hair dryer. It also hurts a little when her thick fingers smooth my hair. Lala decided to be a Brazilian woman years ago, but she was born a Uruguayan man. Now she's the best transvestite stylist in the neighborhood and she doesn't work the streets anymore; faking a Brazilian accent was useful in seducing men when she was hooking, but it doesn't really make sense now. Still, she's so used to it that sometimes she talks on the phone in Portuguese, or she gets mad and raises her arms to the sky and begs for vengeance or mercy from Pomba Gira, her personal spirit, to whom she has a small altar set up in the corner of the room where she cuts hair. It's right next to her computer, which is always lit up in a perpetual chat.

"So you think she's a monster too."

"She gives me the chills, *mami*. It's like she's cursed or something, I don't know."

"Why do you say that?"

"I'm not saying anything. But around here the word is she'll do anything for money. She even goes to witches' sabbats."

"Oh, Lala, what witches? There's no such thing as witches. You shouldn't believe everything you hear."

She gives my hair a yank that seems intentional, but then she apologizes. It was intentional.

"What do you know about what *really* goes on around here, *mamita*? You live here, but you're from a different world."

She's right, even though I don't like to hear it. Nor do I like that she can so candidly put me right in my place: the middle-class woman who thinks she's a rebel because she chose to live in the most dangerous neighborhood in Buenos Aires. I sigh.

"You're right, Lala. But I mean, she lives in front of my house and she's always there, on the mattresses. She never moves."

"You work long hours, you don't know what she does. You don't watch her at night, either. The people in this neighborhood, *mami*, they're really . . . what's the word? You don't even realize and they attack you."

"Stealthy?"

"That's it. You've sure got a vocabulary on you. Doesn't she, Sarita? Real high class, this one."

Sarita has been waiting around fifteen minutes for Lala to finish my hair, but she doesn't mind. She's leafing through magazines. Sarita is a very young transvestite who works the streets above Solís, and she's beautiful.

"Tell her, Sarita, tell her what you told me."

But Sarita pouts her lips like a silent-movie diva; she doesn't feel like telling me anything. It's better that way. I don't want to hear the neighborhood horror stories, which are all unthinkable and plausible at the same time and don't scare me a bit. At least not during the day. At night, if I'm up late to finish a project, and everything is silent so I can concentrate, sometimes I recall the stories they tell in low voices. And I check to be sure the front door is good and locked, and the door to the balcony, too. And sometimes I stand there looking out at the street, especially at the corner where the dirty kid is sleeping beside his mom, both completely still, like nameless dead.

ONE NIGHT AFTER DINNER, the doorbell rang. Strange: almost no one comes to see me at that hour. Only Lala, on nights when she feels lonely and we stay up together listening to sad *rancheras* and drinking whiskey. When I looked out the window to see who it was—no one opens the door right away in this neighborhood, especially when it's nearly midnight—I saw the dirty kid standing there. I ran to get the keys and let him in. He'd been crying; you could tell from the clean streaks down his grubby face. He came running in, but he stopped before he got to the dining room door, as if he needed my permission. Or as if he were afraid to keep going.

"What's wrong?" I asked.

"My mom didn't come back," he said.

His voice was less hoarse now, but he didn't sound like a five-year-old child.

"She left you alone?"

He nodded.

"Are you scared?"

"I'm hungry," he replied. He was scared, too, but he was already hardened and wouldn't acknowledge it in front of a stranger. One who, moreover, had a house, a beautiful and enormous house right there beside his little piece of concrete.

"OK," I told him. "Come on."

He was barefoot. The last time I'd seen him, he'd been wearing some fairly new running shoes. Had he taken them off in the heat? Or had someone stolen them in the night? I didn't want to ask. I sat him down on a kitchen chair and put a little chicken and rice into the oven. While we waited, I spread cheese on some delicious homemade bread. He ate while looking me in the eyes, very seriously, calmly. He was hungry, but not starved.

"Where did your mom go?"

He shrugged.

"Does she leave you alone a lot?"

He shrugged again. I felt like shaking him, and right away I was ashamed. He needed my help; there was no reason for him to satisfy my morbid curiosity. And even so, something about his silence made me angry. I wanted him to be a friendly, charming boy, not this sullen, dirty kid who ate his chicken and rice slowly, savoring every bite, and belched after finishing his glass of Coca-Cola. This he did drink greedily, and then he asked for more. I didn't have anything to give him for dessert, but I knew the ice cream parlor over on the avenue would be open; in summer they served until after midnight. I asked him if he wanted to go, and he said yes with a smile that changed his face completely. He had small teeth, and one on the bottom was about to fall out. I was a little scared to go out so late, and to the avenue, no less. But the ice cream shop tended to be neutral territory; you almost never heard of muggings or fights there.

I didn't bring my purse. Instead I stuffed a little money in the pocket of my jeans. In the street, the dirty kid gave me his hand, and not with the indifference he had when he greeted the people on the subway who bought his prayer cards. He held on tight—maybe he was still scared. We crossed the street, and I saw that the mattress where he slept beside his mother was still empty. The backpack wasn't there, either; she had taken it, or someone had stolen it when they found it there without its owner.

We had to walk three blocks to the ice cream parlor and I decided to take Ceballos, a strange street that could be silent and calm on some nights. The less chiseled transvestites worked there, the chubbiest and oldest ones. I was sorry not to have any shoes to put on the dirty kid's feet. The sidewalks often had shards of glass from broken bottles, and I didn't want him to get hurt. But he walked confidently and seemed used to going barefoot. That night the three blocks were almost empty of transvestites, but they were full of altars. I remembered what they were celebrating: it was January 8, the day of Gauchito Gil, a popular saint from the provinces of Corrientes who has devotees all over the country. He's especially beloved in poor neighborhoods, though you'll see altars all over the city, even in cemeteries. Antonio Gil, it's said, was murdered at the end of the nineteenth century for being a deserter. A policeman killed him, hanged him from a tree and slit his throat. But before he died, the outlaw gaucho told the policeman: "If you want your son to get better, you must pray for me." The policeman did, because his son was very sick. And the boy got better. Then the policeman went back, took Antonio Gil down from the tree, and gave him a proper burial. The place where he had bled to death became a shrine that still exists today, and thousands of people visit it every summer.

I found myself telling the dirty kid the story of the miraculous gaucho, and we stopped in front of one of the altars. There was the plaster saint, with his blue shirt and the red bandanna around his neck—a red headband, too—and a cross on his back, also red. There were many red cloths and a small red flag: the color of blood, in memory of the injustice and the slit throat. But there was nothing macabre or sinister about it. The gaucho brings luck, he cures people, he helps them and doesn't ask them for much in return, just these tributes and sometimes a little alcohol. People make pilgrimages to the Mercedes sanctuary in Corrientes in fifty-degree heat; the pilgrims come on foot, by bus, on horseback, and from all over, even Patagonia. The candles around him made him wink in the half-dark. I lit one that had gone out and then used the flame to light a cigarette. The dirty kid seemed uneasy.

"We're going to the ice cream shop now," I told him. But that wasn't it.

"The gaucho is good," he said. "But the other one isn't."

He said it in a quiet voice, looking at the candles.

"What other one?" I asked.

"The skeleton," he said. "There are skeletons back there."

Around the neighborhood, "back there" always means the other side of the station, past the platforms, where the tracks and the embankment disappear southward. Back there, you often see shrines to saints a little less friendly than Gauchito Gil. I know that Lala goes there to bring offerings to Pomba Gira, colored plates and chickens she buys at the supermarket because she can't get up the nerve to kill one herself. She only goes as far as the embankment, and only during the day, because it can be dangerous. And she told me that "back there" she's seen a lot of shrines to San la Muerte, the skeleton saint of death, with his red and black candles.

"But death's not a bad saint, either," I told the dirty kid, who looked at me with widened eyes as if I were saying something crazy. "He's a saint that can do bad things if people ask him to, but most people don't ask for evil things; they ask for protection. Does your mother bring you back there?" I asked him.

"Yes. But sometimes I go alone," he replied. And then he tugged at my arm to urge me on toward the ice cream shop.

It was really hot. The sidewalk in front of the shop was sticky from so many ice cream cones dripping onto it. I thought about the dirty kid's bare feet, now with all this new grime. He went running in and his old-man's voice asked for a large ice cream with two scoops, chocolate and dulce de leche with chocolate chips. I didn't order anything. The heat took away my appetite, and I was worried about what I should do with the boy if his mother didn't turn up. Bring him to the police station? To a hospital? Let him stay at my house until she came back? Did this city even have anything like social services? There was a number to call in winter to report someone living on the street who was suffering too much from the cold. But that was pretty much all I knew. I realized, while the dirty kid was licking his sticky fingers, how little I cared about people, how natural these desperate lives seemed to me.

When the ice cream was gone, the dirty kid got up from the bench we'd been sitting on and went walking toward the corner where he lived with his mother, practically ignoring me. I followed him. The street was very dark; the electricity had gone out, as often happened on very hot nights. But I could see him clearly in the headlights of the cars. He was also lit, him and his now completely black feet, by the candles in the makeshift shrines. We reached the corner without him taking my hand again or saying a word to me.

His mother was on the mattress. Like all addicts she had no notion of temperature, and she was wearing a thick coat with the hood up, as if it were raining. Her enormous belly was bare, her shirt too short to cover it. The dirty kid greeted her and sat down on the mattress. She said nothing to him.

When she saw me, she was rabid. She ran at me snarling, there's no other way to describe the sound she made. She reminded me of my dog when it broke its hip and went mad with the pain, when it stopped whining and would only growl.

"Where did you take him, you fucking bitch? What do you want with him, huh? Huh? Don't you even think about touching my son!"

She was so close I could see every one of her teeth. I could see that her gums were bleeding, her lips burned by the pipe, and I could smell the tar on her breath.

"I bought him an ice cream," I shouted at her, but I retreated when I saw she had a broken bottle in her hand and was ready to attack me with it.

"Get out of here or I'll cut you, you fucking bitch!"

The dirty kid was staring at the ground as if nothing were happening, as if he didn't know us, not his mother or me. I was furious with him. *Ungrateful little brat,* I thought, and I took off running. I went into my house as fast as I could, though my hands were shaking and I had trouble finding the key. I turned on all the lights—luckily the electricity hadn't gone out on my block. I was afraid the mother might send someone after me to beat me up. Who knew what could be going through her head, or what kinds of friends she had in the neighborhood. I didn't know anything about her. After a while, I went up to the second floor and looked out from the balcony. She was lying there faceup, smoking a cigarette. The dirty kid was next to her and it looked like he was sleeping. I went to bed with a book and a glass of water, but I couldn't read or pay attention to the TV. The heat seemed more intense with the fan on; it only stirred the hot air and drowned out the noise from outside.

In the morning, I forced myself to have breakfast before I went to work. The heat was already suffocating and the sun was barely up. When I closed the door, the first thing I noticed was the absence of the mattress on the corner in front of my house. There was nothing left of the dirty kid or his mother, not a bag or a stain on the pavement or even a cigarette butt. Nothing. Like they'd never even been there.

The body turned up a week after the dirty kid and his mother disappeared. When I came back from work, my feet swollen from the heat, dreaming only of the coolness of my house with its high ceilings and large rooms that not even the most hellish summer could heat up entirely, I found the whole block gone crazy. Three police cars, yellow tape cordoning off a crime scene, and a lot of people crowded just outside its perimeter. It wasn't hard to pick Lala out from the crowd, with her white high heels and gold bun. She was so agitated she'd forgotten to put the false lashes on her right eye and her face looked asymmetrical, almost paralyzed on one side.

"What happened?"

"They found a little kid."

"Dead?"

"Worse. Decapitated! Do you have cable, sweets?"

Lala's cable had been cut off months ago because she hadn't paid the bill. We went into my house and lay on the bed to watch TV, with the ceiling fan spinning dangerously fast and the balcony window open so we could hear if anything interesting happened out on the street. I set a tray on the bed with a pitcher of cold orange juice, and Lala commandeered the remote control. It was strange to see our neighborhood on the screen, to hear the journalists out the window as they dashed back and forth, to look out and see the vans from all the different stations. It was strange to decide to wait for the TV to give us details about the crime, but we knew the neighborhood's dynamics well: no one was going to talk, they wouldn't tell the truth, at least not for the first few days. Silence first, in case any of the people involved in the crime deserved loyalty. Even if it was a horrible child murder. First, mouths shut. In a few weeks the stories would start. Now it was the TV's moment.

Early on, around eight o'clock, when Lala and I were at the start of a long night that began with orange juice, continued with pizza and beer, and ended with whiskey—I opened a bottle my father had given me—information was scarce. In a deserted parking lot on Calle Solís, a dead child had turned up. Decapitated. They'd found the head to one side of the body.

By ten o'clock, we knew that the head was skinned to the bone and that the scalp hadn't been found on the scene. Also, the eyelids had been sewn shut and the tongue bitten, though they didn't know whether by the dead boy himself or—and this brought a shriek from Lala—by someone else's teeth.

The news programs continued with information all night

long, journalists working in shifts, reporting live from the street. The police, as usual, didn't say anything in front of the cameras, but they supplied constant information to the press.

At midnight, no one had claimed the body. It was also known by then that the boy had been tortured: the torso was covered in cigarette burns. They suspected a sexual assault, which was confirmed around two in the morning, when the first forensics report was leaked.

And at that hour, still, no one was claiming the body. No family members. Not a mother or a father or brothers or sisters or uncles or cousins or neighbors or acquaintances. No one.

The decapitated boy, said the TV, was between five and seven years old. It was difficult to calculate because when he was alive he'd been undernourished.

"I want to see him," I told Lala.

"You're crazy! How could they show a decapitated boy? Why would you want to see him? You're morbid. You've always been a little freak, the morbid countess in her palace on Virreyes."

"Lala, I think I know him."

"You know who, the child?"

I said yes and started to cry. I was drunk, but I was also sure that the dirty kid was now the decapitated kid. I told Lala about our encounter the night he'd rung my doorbell. Why didn't I take care of him, why didn't I figure out how to take him away from his mother, why didn't I at least give him a bath? I have a big old beautiful tub and I barely ever use it, I just take quick showers, and only every once in a while do I enjoy an actual bath . . . why didn't I at least wash the dirt off him? And, I don't know, buy him a rubber duck and one of those wands to blow bubbles and let him play? I could easily have bathed him, and then we could have gone for ice cream. Yes, it was late, but there are big supermarkets in the city that never close and they sell tennis shoes, and I could have bought him a pair. How could I have let him walk around barefoot, at night, on these dark streets? I should never have let him go back to his mother. When she threatened me with the bottle I should have called the police, and they'd have thrown her in jail and I'd have kept the boy or helped him get adopted by a family who'd love him. But no. I got mad at him for being ungrateful, for not defending me from his mother! I got mad at a terrified child, son of an addict, a five-year-old boy who lives on the street!

Who *lived* on the street, because now he's dead, decapitated!

Lala helped me throw up in the toilet, and then she went out to buy pills for my headache. I vomited from drunkenness and fear and also because I was sure it was him, the dirty kid, raped and decapitated in a parking lot. And for what?

"Why did they do this to him, Lala?" I asked, curled up in her strong arms, back in bed again, both of us slowly smoking early-morning cigarettes.

"Princess, I don't know if it's really your kid they killed, but we'll go to the DA's office once it's open, so you can get some peace."

"You'll go with me?"

"Of course."

"But why, Lala, why would they do such a thing?"

Lala crushed out her cigarette on a plate next to the bed and poured herself another glass of whiskey. She mixed it with Coca-Cola and stirred it with a finger.

"I don't think it's your boy. The one they killed . . . They had no pity. It's a message for someone."

"A narco's revenge?"

"Only the narcos kill like that."

We were silent. I was scared. There were narcos in Constitución? Like the ones that shocked me when I read about Mexico, ten headless bodies hanging from a bridge, six heads thrown from a car onto the steps of the parliament building, a common grave with seventy-three bodies, some decapitated, others missing arms? Lala smoked in silence and set the alarm. I decided to skip work so I could go straight to the DA and report everything I knew about the dirty kid.

IN THE MORNING, my head still pounding, I made coffee for us both, Lala and me. She asked to use the bathroom. I heard her turn on the shower and I knew she'd be in there at least an hour. I turned on the TV again. The newspaper had no new information. I wasn't going to find anything online, either—the web would only be a boiling cauldron of rumors and insanity.

The morning news said that a woman had come in to claim the decapitated boy. A woman named Nora, who had come to the morgue with a newborn baby in her arms and accompanied by some other family members. When I heard that about the "newborn baby" my heart pounded in my chest. It was definitely the dirty kid, then. The mother hadn't gone sooner for the body because—what a terrible coincidence—the night of the crime had been the night she gave birth. It made sense. The dirty kid had been left alone while his mother delivered and then . . .

Then what? If it was a message, if it was revenge, it couldn't be directed at that poor woman who had slept in front of my house so many nights, that addict girl who couldn't be much older than twenty. Maybe at his father: that's it, his father. Who could the dirty kid's father be?

But then the cameras went crazy, the cameramen running, the journalists out of breath, everyone surging toward the woman coming out of the DA's office. "Nora, Nora," they yelled. "Who could have done this to Nachito?"

"His name is Nacho," I whispered.

And then there she was on the screen, Nora, a close-up of her sobbing and wailing. And it wasn't the dirty kid's mother. It was a completely different woman. A woman around thirty years old, already graying, dark-skinned and very fat—surely the kilos she'd put on with the pregnancy. Almost the opposite of the dirty kid's mother.

It was impossible to make out what she was shouting. She was falling down. Someone, probably a sister, supported her from behind. I changed channels, but they were all showing that wailing woman, until a policeman got between the microphones and her sobs, and a patrol car appeared to take her away. There was a lot of news. I told it all to Lala, sitting on the toilet while she shaved, fixed her makeup, pulled her hair into a neat bun.

"His name is Ignacio. Nachito. And the family had reported him missing on Sunday, but when they saw what was happening on TV, they didn't think it was their son because this boy, Nachito, disappeared in Castelar. They're from Castelar."

"But that's so far away! How did he end up here? Ay, princess, what a fright this all is. I'm canceling all my appointments, it's decided. You can't cut hair after this."

"His belly button was sewn shut, too."

"Whose, the child's?"

"Yes. It seems they tore off his ears, too."

"Princess, no one's ever getting to sleep again around here, I'm telling you. We may be criminals, but this is satanic."

"That's what they're saying. That it's satanic. No, not satanic. They say it was a sacrifice, an offering to San la Muerte."

"Save us, Pomba Gira! Save us, Maria Padilha!"

"Last night I told you the boy talked to me about San la Muerte. It's not him, Lala, but he knew." Lala kneeled in front of me and stared at me with her big dark eyes.

"You, my dear, aren't going to say a word about this. Nothing. Not to the police or anyone. I was crazy last night to think of letting you talk to the judge. Not a word about any of it. We're silent as a grave, pardon the expression."

I listened to her. She was right. I didn't have anything to say, nothing to report. Just a nighttime walk with a boy from the street who disappeared, as street kids often do. Their parents change neighborhoods and take them along. They join groups of child thieves or windshield washers on the avenue, or they become drug mules; when they're being used to sell drugs, they have to change neighborhoods often. Or they set up camp in subway stations. Street kids are never in one place for long; they can stay for a while, but they always leave. Sometimes they run away from their parents. Or they vanish because some distant uncle turns up and takes pity on them and brings them home with him far away in the south, to live in a house on a dirt road and share a room with five other kids, but at least there's a roof over their heads. It wasn't strange, not at all, that the mother and child had disappeared from one day to the next. The parking lot where the decapitated boy had appeared was not on the route the dirty kid and I had taken that night. And the part about San la Muerte? Coincidence. Lala said the neighborhood was full of people who worshipped San la Muerte. All the Paraguayan immigrants and transplants from Corrientes were followers of the saint, but that didn't make them murderers. Lala worshipped Pomba Gira, who looks like a demonic woman, with horns and trident. Did that make her a satanic killer?

It did not.

"I want you to stay with for me a few days, Lala."

"But of course, princess. I'll ready my chambers."

Lala loved my house. She liked to put on music very loud and slowly descend the stairs wearing a turban and holding a cigarette: a femme fatale. "I'm Josephine Baker," she'd say, and then she would complain about being the only transvestite in Constitución who had the faintest idea who Josephine Baker was. "You can't imagine how rough these new girls are, ignorant and empty as a drainpipe. They get worse and worse. It's hopeless."

It was hard to walk around the neighborhood with the same confidence I'd had before the crime. Nachito's murder had an almost narcotic effect on that area of Constitución. At night you didn't hear fighting anymore, and the dealers had moved a few blocks south. There were too many cops watching the place where they'd found the body. Which, said the newspapers and the investigators, had not been the scene of the crime. Someone had dumped him there in the old parking lot, already dead.

On the corner where the dirty kid and his mom used to sleep, the neighbors set up a shrine to the Headless Boy, as they now called him. And they put up a photo with a caption that said *Justice for Nachito.* In spite of the seemingly good intentions, the detectives didn't entirely believe the consternation around the neighborhood. Quite the opposite: they thought people were covering for someone. And so the district attorney had ordered many of the neighbors to be questioned.

I was one of the people they called in to give a statement. I didn't tell Lala, so she wouldn't worry. She hadn't been summoned. It was a very short interview and I didn't say anything that could help them.

I'd slept soundly that night.

No, I hadn't heard anything.

There are street kids in the neighborhood, yes.

The DA showed me the photo of Nachito. I told her I'd never seen him. I wasn't lying. He was completely different from the boys in the neighborhood: a round little boy with dimples and neatly combed hair. I had never seen a boy like that (and smiling!) around Constitución.

No, I never saw black-magic altars in the street or in any of the houses. Only shrines to Gauchito Gil. On Calle Ceballos.

Did I know that Gauchito Gil had practically been decapitated himself, his throat slit? Yes, the whole country knew the legend. I don't think this has to do with Gauchito, do you?

No, of course, you don't have to answer my questions. Well, anyway, I don't think they're related, but I don't know anything about those rituals.

I work as a graphic designer. For a newspaper. For the supplement "Fashion & Woman." Why do I live in Constitución? It's my family's house and it's a beautiful house; you can see it if you go to the neighborhood.

Of course I'll let you know if I hear anything, sure. Yes, I have trouble sleeping, like everyone. We're very scared.

It was clear I wasn't a suspect, they just had to talk to people in the neighborhood. I went home by bus to avoid the five blocks I'd have to walk if I took the subway. Since the murder I'd avoided the subway because I didn't want to run into the dirty kid. And at the same time, my desire to see him again was obsessive, feverish. In spite of the photos, in spite of the evidence—even the pictures of the corpse, which one newspaper had published to the false outrage and horror of a public that bought up every copy of several editions with the decapitated boy on the front page—I still believed it was the dirty kid who had died.

Or who would be the next to die. It wasn't a rational idea. I told it to Lala at her hair salon the afternoon I went back to dye my tips pink again, a job that took hours. Now no one was flipping through magazines or painting their nails or sending text messages while they waited their turn in Lala's chair. Now they did nothing but talk about the Headless Boy. The time of prudent silence had passed, but I still hadn't heard anyone name a suspect in anything but the most general way. Sarita was telling how once, in Chaco, where she was from, a similar thing had happened, only to a little girl.

"They found her with her head off to one side, too, and very raped, poor little soul. She'd shit all over herself."

"Sarita, please, I'm begging you," said Lala.

"But that's how it was, what do you want me to say? We're talking witches, here."

"The police think they're narcos," I said.

"Witch-narcos are everywhere," said Sarita. "You can't even imagine what it's like out in Chaco. They perform rites to ask for protection. That's why they cut off the head and put it to the left of the body. They think if they make those offerings the police won't catch them, because the heads have power. They're not just narcos, they also traffic women."

"But, you think they're around here, in Constitución?"

"They're everywhere," said Sarita.

I dreamed about the dirty kid. I went out onto the balcony and he was in the middle of the street. I waved my arms at him, trying to get him to move because a truck was barreling toward him. But the dirty kid kept looking up, looking at me and the balcony, smiling, his teeth scummy and small. And the truck ran him over and I couldn't help seeing how the wheel burst his belly open like a soccer ball and then dragged his intestines as far as the corner. In the middle of the street was the dirty kid's head, still smiling, his eyes open.

I woke up sweating and shaking. From the street came the sound of a sleepy *cumbia* rhythm. Little by little, some of the neighborhood's noises were coming back: the drunk fighting, the music, the motorcycles with their rattling exhaust pipes—the local kids liked to loosen them so they'd make a lot of noise. There was a gag order on the investigation, which is to say the confusion was absolute. I visited my mother several times and when she asked me to go live with her, for a while at least, I said no. She called me crazy and we argued, yelling at each other like we never had before.

ONE NIGHT I CAME home late because, after the office, I'd gone to a colleague's birthday party. It was one of the last days of summer. I took the bus home and got off before my stop so I could take a walk through the neighborhood, alone. By then I knew how to handle myself again. If you know what you're doing, Constitución is easy. I was smoking as I walked. Then I saw her.

The dirty kid's mother was thin; she'd always been thin, even when she was pregnant. From behind, no one would have guessed at the belly she'd had. It's the usual build of addicts: the hips stay narrow like they're refusing to make room for the baby, the body doesn't produce fat, the thighs don't expand. At nine months, the legs are two rickety sticks holding up a basketball, a woman who swallowed a basketball. Now, without her belly, the dirty kid's mother looked more than ever like a teenager as she leaned against a tree, trying to light her crack pipe under the streetlight, unconcerned about the police—who'd been patrolling the neighborhood much more frequently since the Headless Boy's murder—or about other addicts or anything else.

I approached her slowly, and when she saw me, there was immediate recognition in her eyes. Immediate! Her eyes narrowed, squinted: she wanted to run away, but something stopped her. Maybe she was dizzy. Those seconds of doubt were enough for me to block her escape, to stop in front of her, force her to talk. I pushed her against the tree and held her there. She wasn't strong enough to fight back.

"Where is your son?"

"What son? Let me go."

We both spoke quietly.

"Your son. You know very well who I'm talking about."

The dirty kid's mother opened her mouth and it nauseated me to smell her hungry breath, sweet and rotten like fruit left out in the sun, mixed with the medicinal smell of the drug and that burned stench. Addicts smell of burned rubber, of toxic factories, polluted water, chemical death.

"I don't have any kids."

I pressed her harder against the tree, I grabbed her neck. I don't know if she felt pain, but I drove my nails into her. She wouldn't remember me in a few hours anyway. I wasn't afraid of the police either. I knew they wouldn't get too worried over a fight between two women.

"You're going to tell me the truth. You were pregnant until recently."

The dirty kid's mom tried to burn me with her lighter, but I saw her coming, the thin hand that tried to hold the flame to my hair. The bitch wanted to set me on fire. I squeezed her wrist so hard that the lighter fell to the sidewalk. She stopped fighting.

"I DON'T HAVE ANY KIDS!" she yelled at me, and the sound of her voice, too thick, ill, woke me up. What was I doing? Strangling a dying teenager in front of my house? Maybe my mother was right. Maybe I did need to move. Maybe, as everyone had said, I was fixated on that house because it allowed me to isolate myself, because no one visited me there, because I was depressed and I made up romantic stories about a neighborhood that really was just shit, shit, shit. That was what my mother had shouted at me and I swore never to speak to her again, but now, with my hands around the young addict's neck, I thought maybe she wasn't entirely wrong.

Maybe I wasn't the princess in her castle; maybe I was a madwoman locked in her tower.

The junkie girl wiggled out of my hands and started to run, slowly, still choking. But when she got halfway down the block, right where the streetlight shone directly on her, she turned around. She was laughing and in the light you could see her bleeding gums.

"I gave them to *him*!" she shouted.

The words were for me. She was looking me right in the eyes with that horrible recognition. And then she caressed her belly with both hands and said, clearly, loudly:

"This one too. I promised him them both."

I ran toward her, but she was fast. Or she'd suddenly become fast, I don't know. She crossed Plaza Garay like a cat and I went after her, but when the traffic started moving on the avenue, she managed to dodge the cars and make it across and I didn't.

I couldn't breathe. My legs were shaking. Someone came up to me and asked if the girl had robbed me and I said yes, hoping they'd chase her. But no. They only asked me if I was OK, if I wanted a taxi, what had she stolen from me.

A taxi, yes, I said. I stopped one and asked the driver to take me to my house, only five blocks away. The driver didn't complain. He was used to that kind of short trip in this neighborhood. Or maybe he just didn't feel like arguing. It was late. It must have been his last fare before heading home.

When I closed the door I didn't feel the relief of the cool rooms, the wooden staircase, the walled garden, the old mosaics and high ceilings. I turned on the light and the lamp flickered: *it's going to go out,* I thought, *I'll be left in the dark.* It steadied, though the light it gave off was yellowish, old, dim. I sat down on the floor with my back against the door. I was waiting to hear the soft taps from the dirty kid's sticky hand, or the sound of his head rolling down the stairs. I was waiting for the dirty kid to ask me, again, to let him in.

# The Inn

The cigarette smoke was making her ill, as always when her mother smoked in the car. But today she didn't dare ask her to put it out, because her mother was in a very bad mood. She exhaled the smoke through her nose and it blew into Florencia's eyes. In the backseat her sister Lali was listening to music with her earphones jammed into her ears. No one spoke. Florencia looked out the window at the mansions along Los Sauces and waited eagerly for the tunnel and the dam and the colored hills. She never tired of the landscape even though she saw it several times a year, every time they went to the house in Sanagasta to escape the summer heat.

This trip was different; it wasn't for pleasure, and it wasn't summer. Her father had practically driven them out of La Rioja. Florencia had heard them arguing the night before, and by morning the decision was made: until the elections—Florencia's father was running for La Rioja's city council—the girls and their mother would stay in Sanagasta. The problem was Lali. She went out every weekend and got drunk and had a lot of boyfriends. Lali was fifteen and had straight, dark hair that fell below her waist. She was beautiful, although she really shouldn't use so much makeup, and she should lose the long painted nails and learn to walk in heels already. Florencia watched her in her new boots and laughed at how she walked so crooked and slow. She thought the blue shadow Lali used on her eyelids was ridiculous, not to mention those horrible pearl earrings, but she understood why men liked her, and why her father didn't want her running around La Rioja during the campaign. Florencia had often had to defend her sister after school, and sometimes things came to blows. *Your sister the whore, the skank, the dicklicker, cocksucker, has she taken it up the ass yet, or what?* It was always the girls who insulted Lali. Once, Florencia had gone home with a split lip after a fight in the plaza. While she was washing up in the bathroom and thinking of a lie to tell her parents—that she'd gotten a ball in the face at volleyball practice—she felt like an idiot. Her sister never thanked her for defending her. She never talked to her at all, really. She didn't care what people said about her, she didn't care that Florencia stuck up for her, she didn't care about Florencia. She spent all her time in her room trying on clothes and listening to stupid music, crappy love songs, *vas a verme llegar, you'll see me coming, you'll hear my song, you'll enter without asking for the key . . .* the same sappy song all day, it was enough to make you want to kill her. Florencia didn't like her sister, but she couldn't help getting mad when people called her a slut. She didn't like it when they called anyone a slut; she would have fought for anyone.

No one was ever going to call Florencia a slut, she knew that for sure. She rolled down the window to get a better look at the dam and the Gypsy's Skirt, that part of the hill that looked like the stain from a now-dry waterfall of blood. Her mouth filled with barely damp air. No, they'd call her carpet-muncher, freak, sicko, who knew what else.

"Mom, can you put some music on? My batteries ran out," said Lali.

"Don't bug me, kiddo, my head's splitting and I have to drive."

"Ugh, you're so lame."

"Shut up, Lali, or I'll smack you."

*So this is what it's come to*, thought Florencia. Her mother didn't like Sanagasta. Like many people from La Rioja she went to the town in summer, when the heat in the province's capital rose to fifty degrees and there was no sleeping during siesta and you just wanted to die. She always talked about going to Uspallata instead, or to the beach. She said she was sick of Sanagasta; there were no restaurants, the people were sullen and hostile, and in the craft market the wares never changed—they didn't even move things around! She was sick of the procession of the Virgin Child, of the little shrines everywhere, of the fact that there were three churches and not a single place to drink a cup of coffee. If someone told her there was coffee at the Inn, she got riled up as well. She was sick of the Inn. Sick of its owner, Elena, whose excessive friendliness struck her as false and conceited. Sick of how the only entertainment was to go and eat baked chicken at the Inn, play roulette and the slot machines at the Inn's casino, talk to some European tourist at the Inn. It was lucky, she'd often say, that they had a swimming pool at their house; otherwise they'd have had to use the one at the Inn, and then she'd really go crazy. Not even a steak house in the whole town, she complained. Not a single steak house.

They reached Sanagasta at the same time as the first evening bus, around six thirty. The low-hanging sun had changed the color of the hills, and the green of the valley's trees was a velvety moss. Lali was crying. She hated Sanagasta and she was so angry, so convinced that when high school finished she would run away to Córdoba, where one of her boyfriends lived . . . Florencia had learned of the escape plan when Lali told a girlfriend about it over the phone.

The house was fairly cool and her mother, who always felt cold, lit the heater. Florencia went out to the yard. Her family's vacation house was small because her father had opted for a large plot of land so they could have a pool, trees, a lot of space for the dogs to run, a gazebo, and even flowers. Her father loved flowers, much more than her mother, who preferred cacti. Florencia flopped into the hammock-chair and started to observe the colors: the rust-orange and fuchsia flowers, the turquoise of the pool, prickly pear green, the coral-pink of the house. She sent a message to her best friend, Rocío, who lived in Sanagasta: *I'm here, come meet me.* They had a lot to talk about: Rocío had told her in an email that she was having family problems, too. That is, she had problems with her father, because Rocío's family was minimal: her mother was dead and she didn't have any siblings. Rocío messaged that they should meet at the kiosk, which was open by then, and without telling anyone Florencia went running out, a little money in her pocket so she could drink a Coca-Cola. Of all the things she liked about Sanagasta, one of her favorites was being able to come, without her parents getting angry or scared.

There was a smell of burning in the air, probably a bonfire of fallen leaves. It was the nicest moment of the day. Rocío was waiting for her, sitting in one of the plastic chairs at the kiosk where they served sandwiches and empanadas at night. She was wearing frayed jean shorts and a white shirt, and her backpack was under the table. Florencia kissed her on the cheek and sat down, and as she did she couldn't help glancing at her friend's legs, their golden down that in the afternoon light looked like spilled wax. They ordered a two-liter Coke, and Florencia told Rocío to spill everything.

For years, Rocío's father had worked at the Inn as a tour guide: he brought the guests to the archaeological park, to the dam, and to the Salamanca cave, where he told them ghost stories about meetings between witches and devils, or about stinking, red-eyed goats; furred snakes; and a basilisk with blazing eyes. He was the star employee and was treated accordingly: he used Elena's 4×4 when his truck broke down, he ate free at the restaurant whenever he wanted, he used the pool and the foosball table without paying, and around town people said he was Elena's lover. Rocío denied it, saying her father wouldn't get mixed up with his boss, not that snooty woman. Florencia had gone on all the tours with Rocío and her father. He was an incredible guide, caring and kind: he was so fun that you didn't get tired even though you were climbing hills under a terrible sun.

"I can't believe Elena fired your dad. What happened?"

Rocío wiped the Coca-Cola from her upper lip, a maroon mustache.

Things were going pretty badly, she said, because Elena was having money problems and she was hysterical, but everything went to hell when her father had told some tourists from Buenos Aires about the Inn's past, about how it had been a police academy thirty years ago, before it was turned into a hotel.

"But your dad always says that on the tours when he talks about the town's history," said Florencia.

"Well, yes, but Elena didn't know that. Then these tourists

got really interested. They wanted to know more about it, and they asked Elena directly—about disappearances, torture, whatever. That's how she found out that my dad told the guests about the police academy. They fought, and she fired him."

"But why did she get so mad?"

"She doesn't want the tourists to get a bad impression, my dad says, because it was a police academy during the dictatorship. You remember that stuff we studied in school?"

"What, did they kill people there?"

"My dad says no, Elena is being paranoid. It was just a police academy and nothing more."

Rocío said the thing about the police academy during the dictatorship was an excuse of Elena's, that she didn't really care at all about the story, since she'd only bought the Inn ten years ago. She was just pissed at Rocío's father and wanted to fire him, and she latched onto that as an excuse. Elena had taken away Rocío's father's key to the Inn's front door; she'd asked him for money to fix things on the 4×4 that he hadn't broken, that were just from regular wear and tear; and she'd forbidden him to give tours on his own under threat of suing him. And all without paying him for the last month of work.

"But he can still give tours, she can't stop him."

"He's not going to, he doesn't want to make trouble. Plus, he told me he's fed up with the people in Sanagasta, he wants to leave."

Rocío finished her glass of Coke and whistled to the kiosk's dog, who came right over and seemed disappointed when she petted him instead of giving him food.

"I got so mad at him . . . it would suck to move away. I want to go to school in La Roja, with you and the girls."

The dog had come over to try its luck with Florencia, and

now she leaned down to pet its ears so she could hide her face a little. She didn't want Rocío to see that she was about to start crying; if Rocío left Sanagasta, Florencia would run away with her, she didn't care. But then she heard the best possible news, the best she'd heard in her life.

"So I told him that, I asked him if we could stay. And guess what? He told me we were leaving Sanagasta but only to move to La Rioja. He's already talked to the secretary of tourism about a job. Isn't it great?"

Florencia pressed her lips together and then said it was awesome. She finished her Coca-Cola to swallow her emotion. "Let's go to the rose plaza," said Rocío. "The buds opened, you can't imagine how pretty the flowers are."

The dog went with them, and so did what was left of the Coca-Cola. Night had almost fallen. All the streets in the center of Sangasta were paved and lit. Through the windows of some houses they could see people gathered, many of them women, to pray the rosary. Florencia was a little afraid of those meetings, especially when there were candles lit and the flickering glow illuminated all the faces and their closed eyes. It looked like a funeral. No one prayed in her family. In that, they were very strange.

Rocío sat down on one of the benches and said, "Finally: Flor, now I can tell you. Back at the kiosk it was no good, they might have been listening to us. You've got to help me with something."

"With what?"

"No, first tell me you're going to help me. Swear it."

"OK, I swear."

"OK. Check this out."

Rocío opened the backpack she had carried the whole way

to the plaza and showed her what was inside. When the light from the streetlamp fell onto it, Florencia gave a startled jump: it looked like the meat was a dead animal, a piece of a human body, something macabre. But no: it was uncured chorizo sausages. To relax and to keep Rocío from laughing at her moment of panic, she said, "What do you want me to help you with, a barbecue?"

"No, dummy. It's to scare the shit out of Elena."

Then Rocío explained her plan, and in her eyes it was clear that she hated Elena. She knew, clearly, that Elena had been her father's girlfriend. She knew they had fought over the police academy, but that the real problem was something else. Still, she didn't admit it. It only came through in the way she talked about Elena, the way her voice trembled with happiness when she imagined her humiliated. It was clear she wanted to punish Elena and defend her mother. Florencia focused all her mental energy; someone had told her once that if you wished hard for something you could make it happen, and she wanted Rocío to confide in her, to trust her. If only she would, then they would really be inseparable. But Rocío didn't say another word, and so Florencia just agreed to meet her after dinner behind the Inn, and to bring a flashlight.

THEY COULD GET IN through the gate by the pool, which was always open. Anyway, in Sanagasta no one locked their doors. It was the off-season, so the whole big building that surrounded the pool area was closed. Only the main building was in use, the one that looked out onto the street; in between the two was the casino, which was also closed that time of year except when someone rented it out for a special occasion. The Inn's shape was odd—it really was a lot like a barracks.

Florencia and Rocío went in barefoot so they wouldn't make any noise. They had keys because Rocío's father still had a set for the back door and a copy of the master key for the bedrooms. Rocío figured he'd planned to return them and then forgotten in the heat of the argument. As soon as she saw them, she had the idea: sneak into the Inn at night, when the employee on duty was sleeping in a room in the front building, far away. They'd go into several of the rooms, make holes in the mattresses—which were made of foam: it wouldn't even take a sharp knife to tear them—stick a chorizo inside, and remake the bed. In a couple of months, the smell of decomposing meat would be unbearable, and with luck, it would take them a long time to find the source of the stench. Florencia was surprised by the nastiness of the plan, and Rocío said she'd seen it in a movie.

No sooner did they open the gate than they saw Blackie, the most protective of the Inn's dogs. But Blackie knew Rocío and greeted her by licking her hand. To soothe him further she gave him one of the sausages, and he went off to eat it beside a cactus. They made it inside with no problems. The hallway was very dark and when Florencia turned on the flashlight she felt a savage fear; she was sure the light would illuminate a white face rushing toward her, or that it would betray the feet of a man hiding in a corner. But there was nothing. Nothing but what should have been there: the bedroom doors, some chairs, a sign for the bathrooms, the computer room where the machine was turned off and some framed photos on the walls showed Chaya harvest festivals of years gone by. The Inn always filled up during Chaya, and they threw lively *chayero* parties on the grounds.

Rocío signaled for her to follow. She was very pretty in the dark, thought Florencia. Her hair was pulled back into a pony-tail and she was wearing a black sweater, because night in Sanagasta was always cold. In the silence of the empty building Florencia could hear Rocío's agitated breathing. "I'm crazy nervous," Rocío murmured close to her ear, and she brought Florencia's hand, the one not holding the flashlight, to her chest. "Feel how my heart is pounding." Florencia let Rocío press her hand against that warmth and she had a strange feeling, like she had to pee, a tingling just below her belly button. Rocío let go of her hand and went into one of the rooms, but the feeling stayed with Florencia, and she had to grip the flashlight with both hands because the light was trembling on the wall.

Tearing the mattress with the kitchen knife they'd brought turned out to be easy, just as Rocío had predicted. Nor was it difficult to put the meat into the hole. From the side the knife opening was noticeable, but once they put the sheets back on the trick was perfect. No one would ever guess that there was sausage or anything else hidden in the mattress; at least not right away. They carried out the same operation in two more rooms, and then Florencia, who was starting to get scared, said: "Why don't we go, this is enough."

"No, I still have six chorizos left. Come on," said Rocío, and Florencia had no choice but to follow her.

They went into a room that looked out onto the street. They had to be very careful that the light from the flashlight couldn't be seen from outside, because the shutters over the window weren't closed well. There was even a little light from a street-light shining in. At that hour probably no one would be out in Sanagasta, but you never knew. What if someone thought there were burglars in the Inn and shot at them? Anything could happen. They made the cut, stuffed in the sausage, and remade the bed with no trouble.

"I'm tired," said Rocío. "Let's lie down a while."

"You're crazy."

"Oh, it's fine. Come on, let's take a break."

But when they were about to lie down together on the freshly made double bed, a noise came from outside that made them crouch down, terrified. It was sudden and impossible: the sound of a car or truck, so loud that it couldn't be real, it had to be a recording. And then there was another motor and then someone started pounding on the shutters with something metal and the two girls embraced in the darkness, screaming, and now in addition to the noise of the motors and the pounding on the windows, there were the running steps of many feet thudding around the Inn, and the cries of men, and the men who were running beat on all the windows and the shutters and they shone the headlights of the truck or the car into the room where the girls were; they could see the headlights between the shutter slats. The car had driven up through the garden and the feet kept running and the hands pounding and something metallic was also pounding and they could hear the voices of men, many men, shouting. One of them said, "Let's go, let's go," and then they heard shattering glass and more shouts. Florencia could feel it as she wet herself, she couldn't help it, she couldn't, nor could she keep screaming because the fear wouldn't let her breathe.

The car's headlights turned off and the door to the room opened little by little.

The girls tried to get up, but they were trembling too much. Florencia thought she was going to faint. She hid her face on

Rocío's shoulder and hugged her until it hurt. Two people had come into the room. One of them turned on the light, and the girls barely recognized her: Elena. Beside her was Telma, the night-shift employee. "What are you two doing here?" asked Elena when she had taken in the sight of them, and Telma lowered the gun she was holding. Elena yanked them angrily up from the floor, but then she realized that the girls were too afraid: she had heard them scream like they were being murdered. It was their own screams that had given them away. The girls weren't afraid of her; something else had happened, but Elena couldn't figure out what it was. When she tried to question them, they cried or asked if that had been the Inn's alarm. They asked what that noise had been and who was doing the pounding. "What alarm?" asked Elena several times. "What men are you talking about?" But the girls didn't seem to understand. One of the two, the daughter of the lawyer running for La Rioja's city council, had pissed herself. Mario's daughter had a backpack full of chorizos. What was this, by God? Why had they screamed like that, and for so long? Telma said she had heard them crying and howling for around five minutes.

It was Mario's daughter who spoke first, and more calmly: she said they had heard cars, they'd seen headlights, she talked again about running feet and pounding on the windows. Elena got angry. The brat was lying—she was making that ghost story up to ruin the Inn for her the way Mario had wanted to. She was betraying her the way Mario had, surely on his orders. She didn't want to hear any more. She called the lawyer's wife and Mario; she told them that she'd found the girls in the Inn and asked them to come pick them up. This time she wouldn't call the police, but if it happened again, they'd go straight to the station.

## The Intoxicated Years

1989

ALL THAT SUMMER the electricity went off for six hours at a time; government orders, because the country had no more energy, they said, though we didn't really understand what that meant. Our parents couldn't get over how the Minister of Public Works had announced the measures they were taking to avoid a widespread blackout while in a room lit only by a hurricane lamp: like in a slum, they repeated. What would a widespread blackout be like? Would we be left in the dark forever? The possibility was incredible. Stupid. Ridiculous. Useless adults, we thought, how useless. Our mothers cried in the kitchen because they didn't have enough money or there was no electricity or they couldn't pay the rent or because inflation had eaten away at their salaries until they didn't cover anything beyond bread and cheap meat, but we girls—their daughters—didn't feel sorry for them. Those things all seemed just as stupid and ridiculous as the power outages.

Meanwhile, we had a van. It belonged to Andrea's boyfriend.

Andrea was the prettiest of us, the one who knew how to rip up jeans to make fabulous cutoffs and wore crop tops that she bought with money she stole from her mother. The boyfriend's name doesn't matter. He had a van that he used to deliver groceries during the week, but on weekends it was all ours. We smoked some poisonous pot from Paraguay that smelled like urine and pesticide when it was dry but was cheap and effective. The three of us would smoke, and once we were totally out of our minds we'd get into the back of the van, which didn't have windows or any light at all because it wasn't designed for people, it was made to transport cans of garbanzos and peas. We would have him drive really fast and then slam on the brakes, or go around and around the traffic island at the entrance to the town. We had him speed up around corners and make us bounce over speed bumps. And he did it all because he was in love with Andrea and he hoped that one day she would love him back.

We would scream and tumble on top of each other. It was better than a roller coaster and better than alcohol. Sprawled in the darkness we felt like every blow to the head could be our last, and sometimes, when Andrea's boyfriend had to stop for a red light, we sought each other out in the darkness to be sure we were all still alive. And we roared with laughter, sweaty, sometimes bloody, and the inside of the truck smelled of empty stomachs and onions, and sometimes of the apple shampoo we all shared. We shared a lot: clothes, the hair dryer, bikini wax. People said that we were similar, that the three of us looked alike, but that was just an illusion because we copied each other's movements and ways of speaking. Andrea was beautiful, tall, with thin and separated legs; Paula was too blond and turned a horrible shade of red when she spent too long in the sun; I could never manage a flat belly or thighs that didn't rub together and chafe when I walked.

Andrea's boyfriend would make us get out after an hour, once he got bored or started to worry the police would pull the van over and think that maybe he had kidnapped the three girls in the back. Sometimes he dropped us off at one of our houses, or sometimes in Plaza Italia, where we bought that poisonous Red Dot weed from the hippies in the artisan market. We also drank sangria that one of the hippies made in a five-liter tomato can with giant pieces of fruit because he was lazy and always too drunk to cut the bananas, oranges, and apples into smaller chunks. Once, we found an entire grapefruit, and one of us put it in her mouth like a stuffed Christmas piglet and ran around between the stalls. It was night, and the crafts were illuminated with lights running on a generator that all the vendors shared.

We would go back home very late, hours after the market closed; no one paid any attention to us that summer. The authorities didn't keep to the duration of the power outages, and we spent the longest nights of our lives dying of heat in yards and on sidewalks, listening to the radio using batteries that seemed to run out more and more quickly as the days went by.

## 1990

THEY'D FORCED THE PRESIDENT to hand over the reins before the end of his term, and no one liked the new one too much, even though he'd won the elections by an impressive margin. The stench of resignation was in the air; it seeped from the twisted mouths of the embittered people, including the whiny parents we scorned now more than ever. But the new president had promised that from then on it wouldn't take years to get a telephone line once you requested it; the phone company was so inefficient that some of our neighbors had been waiting a decade for the thing, and sometimes when the technicians showed up to install it—they never called first—there would be impromptu celebrations. Out of pure luck we had telephones, all three of us, and we'd spend hours talking until our parents cut us off, yelling. It was during one of those phone conversations on some Sunday afternoon that Paula decided we had to start going to Buenos Aires. We would lie and say we were going out in our town, but really we would take the early bus on Saturday and spend the night in Buenos Aires. At dawn we'd be back at the station and home in the morning; our parents would never even know.

They never knew.

I fell in love with the waiter in a bar called Bolivia; he rejected me. "I get around," he told me.

"What the hell do I care," I shouted at him, and I downed almost a liter of gin and if I slept with someone else that night I don't remember. When I woke up I was on the bus home; it was already day and my shirt was covered in vomit. I had to go by Andrea's house to wash up before I went to mine. At Andrea's no one ever asked questions; her dad was almost always drunk and she had a lock on her bedroom door so he couldn't get in at night. When we went to her house it was better to stay in the kitchen—her dad only went in there to get more ice for his wine.

In that kitchen we swore an oath that we would never have boyfriends. We swore with blood, cutting ourselves a little, and with kisses, in the dark because once again there was no power. We made the promise while thinking about that drunken father, about what we would do if he came in and found us bleeding and embracing. He was tall and strong but he tended to stagger more than walk, and it would have been easy to push him down. But Andrea didn't want to push him; she was always weak with men. I promised never to fall in love again, and Paula said she was never going to let a man touch her.

One night, when we were on our way back from Buenos Aires earlier than usual, a girl got up from one of the seats in front of us, went up to the driver, and asked him to stop so she could get off. The driver braked in surprise and told her there was no bus stop there. We were going through Parque Pereyra: an enormous park halfway between Buenos Aires and our town. It had once been an estate of over ten thousand hectares that Perón expropriated from its millionaire owners. Now, it's a nature reserve, a damp, sinister little forest where the sun barely enters. The road cuts it right in half. The girl insisted. The passengers started waking up and one man said, "But where do you want to go at this hour, dear?" The girl, who was our age and had her hair pulled back in a ponytail, looked at him with such intense hatred he was struck dumb. She looked at him like a witch, like an assassin, like she had evil powers. The driver let her off and she ran toward the trees; when the bus started up again she disappeared in a cloud of dust. One woman complained aloud: "But how can you leave her out there alone at this hour? Who knows what could happen to her." She and the driver argued almost until we reached the terminal.

We never forgot that girl or her evil look. No one could ever hurt her, we were sure about that; if anyone was going to do harm, it was her. She wasn't carrying a bag or a backpack, we remembered, and her clothes were too light for the coolness of the autumn night.

Once, we went looking for her. Andrea's boyfriend, the one

with the van, had disappeared from our lives, but there was another boy, Paula's brother, who by then could drive his father's car. We didn't know exactly where the girl had gotten off the bus, just that it wasn't too far from the windmill—the park has a Dutch-style windmill that doesn't produce anything, it's just a chocolate shop for tourists. Walking among the trees, we discovered paths and a house that had maybe once been part of the estate. These days it's been refurbished; you can visit it like a museum and they even hold exclusive wedding receptions there. But back then there was just a park ranger who took care of the place, and it seemed to be holding its breath among the pines, secret and empty.

Maybe she's the park ranger's daughter, Paula's brother said, and he brought us home laughing at us, the silly girls who thought they'd seen a ghost.

But I know that girl wasn't anyone's daughter.

1991

HIGH SCHOOL WAS NEVER-ENDING. We started hiding bottles of whiskey in our backpacks and sneaking to the bathroom to drink from them. We also stole Emotival from my mother; Emotival was a pill she took because she was depressed, et cetera. It didn't do anything much to us, just brought on a terrible fatigue, an exhaustion that made us fall asleep in class with our mouths open, snoring. They called in our parents, who thought that since we went to bed very late, our morning comas were caused by a lack of sleep. They were just as stupid as ever, although now they were less nervous about inflation and the lack of money: the government had passed a new law declaring that one peso was equal to a dollar, and although no one entirely believed it, hearing *dollar dollar dollar* filled my parents and all the other adults with happiness.

We were still poor, though. My family rented and Paula's family had a half-finished house, with old-fashioned, interconnected bedrooms. It was disgusting: her brothers were older and she had to walk through their rooms to go to the bathroom; sometimes she saw them masturbating. Andrea's apartment belonged to her family, but they could never pay their bills on time, and when their electricity wasn't getting cut off, their phone was. Her mother couldn't find any work except as an old people's nurse, and her drunk father went on throwing money away on wine and cigarettes.

Even so, we three believed we could be rich. We thought that being rich was something that lay in our future. Until we met Ximena. A new classmate, she came from Patagonia and her parents had something to do with oil. When she invited us over we ran all through the house, bumping into each other as we tried to take it all in at once; we would have taken pictures if we could. The living room had a little bridge over an indoor pond with floating plants, water lilies, algae. None of the rooms had tile floors; they were all made of wood, and paintings hung on the white walls. The backyard had a pool, rosebushes, and white-pebbled paths. Seen from the street the house didn't look all that pretty, but inside it was madness, all those nice things, the scent of perfume in the air, armchairs of colored velveteen and rugs that were neither frayed nor worn. We detested Ximena immediately. She was ugly and had a vertical scar on her chin, and at school they called her buttface because of it. We convinced her to steal money from her mother—it was so easy for her!—and we used it to buy drugs, sometimes pills from the pharmacy. These days they're really strict, but back then if you just told the pharmacist you had an autistic brother or a psychotic father, they would sell you medication without a prescription. We knew the names of some medicines for psychosis, because we wrote them down whenever someone mentioned them. When we took the blue pills that we avoided forever after, poor Ximena went so nuts she tried to set the fine wooden floor of her room on fire, and she went on and on about all the eyes she saw floating around the house. We weren't impressed. The year before, one of the hippies at the artisan market had been put away after he'd eaten too many mushrooms. He said there were tiny men only a few centimeters tall who were shooting little arrows into his neck. He wanted to pull out the imaginary arrows so bad that he scratched at his neck until he almost slashed his jugular with his nails. He'd always wanted to be Paula's boyfriend—he called her his "spiritual companion." Paula stole acid from him to take on our birthdays. He had only a few teeth, and his friends called him Jeremiah. They took him to the psychiatric ward in Romero and nothing more was ever heard from him.

Ximena had to have her stomach pumped and everyone blamed us. We didn't care, except that we'd miss her money. That was when we started hating rich people.

1992

LUCKILY, WE MET ROXANA, the new girl on our street. She was eighteen and lived alone. Her place was at the end of an alley, and we were so skinny we could fit through the bars of the gate if it was locked. Roxana never had food in the house; her empty cupboards were crisscrossed by bugs dying of hunger as they searched for nonexistent crumbs, and her fridge kept one Coca-

Cola and some eggs cold. The lack of food was good; we had promised each other to eat as little as possible. We wanted to be light and pale like dead girls. "We don't want to leave footprints in the snow," we'd say, even though in our town it never snowed.

One time we went into Roxana's house and saw, on the kitchen table and next to the thermos—she always had *yerba mate*—what looked to us like an enormous white orb, the kind a fortune-teller would use, a crystal ball, a mirror of the future. But no: it was cocaine. It belonged to one of her friends. She wanted to do a little before she sold the rest; she thought the buyers wouldn't notice what was missing.

She let us scrape the magic ball with a razor and taught us to snort it off of a ceramic plate, heated with a lighter. That way it wouldn't get damp from the humidity, she explained; it wouldn't stick and went down great. It was great and we were great with the white light in our heads and our tongues numb. We did it at the table and also off the mirror in Roxana's bedroom; she placed it right in the middle and we all sat around it, as if the mirror were a lake where we lowered our heads to drink, and the stained walls with their peeling paint were our forest. We took some with us when we went out, storing the cocaine in the silvered paper of cigarette packs, and sometimes in little plastic bags. I used pens, Paula had her own metal straw, and Andrea preferred to smoke pot because she couldn't stand the racing of her heart; Roxana used rolled-up bills and told lies. She said her cousin had disappeared while exploring the Nazca Lines in Mexico. None of us told her that the Lines were in Peru. She said she had been in an amusement park where every door led to a different room, room after room until you found the right one. There could have been hundreds of rooms—the game took up acres. We didn't tell her we'd read something like that in a kids' book called *The Museum of Dreams.* She said that witches gathered in Parque Pereyra, that they held ceremonies and worshipped a man made of straw, and though we were startled to hear about rituals in the park, we didn't tell her that what she described was a lot like a movie we'd seen on TV one Saturday afternoon, a really great horror movie about killing little girls to bring fertility back to a British island.

Sometimes we didn't do cocaine and instead took a little acid with alcohol. We'd turn off all the lights and play with lit sticks of incense in the darkness; they looked like fireflies and made me cry. They reminded me of a tiled house in a park with a pond where frogs played and lightning bugs flew among the trees.

One afternoon when we were playing with incense, we put on an album, *Ummagumma* by Pink Floyd, and we felt like something was chasing us through the house, maybe a bull or a wild boar with teeth for horns, and we ran and crashed into each other, hurting ourselves. It was like being back in the van again, but this time in a nightmare.

1993

In our last year of high school Andrea found a new boyfriend, the singer of a punk band. She changed. She wore a dog collar around her neck, she tattooed her arms with stars and skulls, and she didn't spend Friday nights with us anymore.

I knew she had slept with him. She smelled different, and sometimes she looked at us with contempt and fake smiles. I told her she was a traitor. I reminded her of Celina, a girl from our school who was a little older than us, and who had died after her fourth abortion, bleeding out in the street as she tried to get to the hospital. Abortion was illegal and the women who performed them kicked the girls right out to the street afterward. There were dogs in the clinics; supposedly the animals ate the fetuses so there would be no trace left behind. She looked at us angrily and said she didn't care if she died. We left her crying in the plaza.

Paula and I were furious, and we decided to take the bus to Parque Pereyra. We were going to look for the girl from the forest again. Could she be our third friend if Andrea abandoned us? By then they'd built the highway and only the worst buses still circulated through the park: the ones with decades of grime stuck to the seats, the ones that smelled of gasoline and sweat, had floors sticky from spilled soda and possibly urine. We got off in the park at sunset. At that hour there were still families there, kids running over the grass, some boys playing football. "What a pain in the ass," said Paula, and we sat down under a pine tree to wait for nightfall. A caretaker came by with a flashlight and asked us if we were leaving.

"Yes," we told him.

"The next bus comes in half an hour," he said. "You'd better go wait by the road."

"We're going," we told him, and I smiled. Paula didn't smile because she was so thin that when she showed her teeth she looked like a skull.

"Be careful of scorpions," he said. "If you feel one bite you, just yell, I'll hear you."

More smiling.

That September, which was exceptionally hot, there was an invasion of scorpions. I thought maybe I could let one of them bite me so I'd die. Maybe that way we'd be remembered like Celina, dead in the street with her bloody fetus between her legs. I lay back on the grass and thought about venom. Paula, meanwhile, walked among the trees asking in a low voice, "Are you there?" She came to get me when she heard a rustling in the trees and saw a white shadow. "Shadows aren't white," I told her. "This one was white," she assured me. We walked until we were exhausted. The lack of energy was the worst thing about quitting eating. It was worth it except for now, when we wanted to find our friend, the girl with eyes full of hate.

We didn't find her. Nor did we get lost; the light from the moon was bright enough to make out the paths leading to the road. Paula found a white ribbon that, she thought, could belong to our friend from Parque Pereyra. "Maybe she left it for us as a message," Paula said. *I don't think so,* I thought. Surely someone who'd been picnicking in the park had lost it, but I didn't say anything because I could see she was convinced, happy with her new amulet, sure it was a sign. I felt a stabbing in my leg that was neither a scorpion nor death; it was a nettle that burned my skin and covered it in bloody red spots.

1994

PAULA CELEBRATED HER BIRTHDAY at Roxana's house. For the party we scored some acid that, we'd been told, had been recently smuggled over from Holland. They called it Little Dragon. Was imported acid stronger? Since we didn't know, just to be safe, we took a little less than usual—just a fourth. We put on a Led Zeppelin album. We knew it was going to piss off Andrea's boyfriend, and that's what we wanted: to piss him off. He arrived when the record was ending. We were still listening to vinyl then, although we could have bought CDs. All electronics were cheap—TVs and stereos, photo and video cameras. It couldn't last long, said my parents, it couldn't be true that an

Argentine peso had the same worth as a dollar. But we were so sick of everything they said: my parents, the other parents, always announcing the end, the catastrophe, the imminent return to blackouts and all the pathetic hardships. Now they didn't cry over inflation; they cried because they didn't have jobs. They cried as if they weren't to blame for any of it. We hated innocent people.

Andrea and her punk boyfriend arrived when the most hippie song on the album was playing, the one about going to California with flowers in your hair, and Andrea's boyfriend scrunched up his face and said, "This sucks, fuckin' stoners." Paula's brother, who was always friendly, offered him a little acid, just a fourth because he didn't want to waste it on the punk. "Acid's hippie, too," Paula's brother said, and the punk said that was true, but since it was chemical and artificial, he liked it. He preferred all things chemical, he said: powdered juices, pills, nylon.

We were in Roxana's room. The mirror was hanging on the wall. There were a lot of people in the house, lots of strangers, as tends to be the case in drug houses: those people whose faces are half seen in a dream as they take beer from the fridge and vomit into the toilet and sometimes steal the key or make some generous gesture, like springing for more drinks when the party is about to end. The acid was like a delicate electric charge. Our fingers trembled; we put our hands in front of our eyes and our nails looked blue. Andrea was back with us, and when we put on *Led Zeppelin III* she wanted to dance, she shouted about lands of ice and snow and about the hammer of the gods, and only in "Since I've Been Loving You," maybe because it was a blues song about love, did she turn around to look at her punk boyfriend. He was sitting in a corner and he looked scared to death. He was pointing at something and repeating who knows what, the music drowned it out. I thought it was funny; there was nothing left of that arrogant, twisted upper lip of his, and he'd taken off his sunglasses too. His pupils were so dilated his eyes were almost black.

I walked slowly over to him and tried to imitate the look of hatred in the eyes of the girl in Parque Pereyra. The electricity made my hair stand on end; I felt like it had turned into wires, or as if it were weightless, like when a TV that's just been turned off attracts your hair so it sticks to the screen.

"Are you scared?" I asked him, and he answered with a confused look. He was cute; that was why Andrea had abandoned us. He was cute and he was innocent. I grabbed his chin and with my other hand I hit him in the face; I punched him right near his temple. His hair, styled so carefully with gel, became a tangled mess hanging over his forehead. Paula, laughing behind me, threw at his head the scissors we'd used to cut strips of acid. Only then did I notice she had the forest girl's white ribbon tied in her hair. It was pure bad luck the scissors hit the punk boyfriend just above his eyebrow, a part of the face that bleeds a lot. We knew this because once in the van we'd cut our foreheads after an especially violent slamming of the brakes. He got scared then, the punk, he got really scared with the blood dripping down over his white shirt, and he must have seen the same thing we did, or something similar distorted by the acid: his hands covered in blood, the stained walls, the three of us surrounding him and holding knives. He tried to run out of the house but he couldn't find the door. Andrea followed him, tried to talk to him, but he couldn't understand her. When he made it out to the patio, the punk boyfriend tripped over a flowerpot, and once on the ground he started to shake—I don't know if he was afraid or having a seizure. The album finished playing but there was no silence; we heard shouting and laughter. Someone was hallucinating scorpions, or maybe they had really infested the house.

We circled the punk boyfriend, looming over him. Lying on the ground with his eyes half closed and his chest covered in blood, he seemed insignificant. He didn't move. Paula slid her knife into her jeans pocket; it was practically a toy, a little knife for spreading jam on bread. "We're not going to need it," she said.

"Is he dead?" asked Andrea, and her eyes shone.

Someone put a new record on back in the house, which seemed so far away. Paula took the ribbon from her hair and tied it around her wrist. Together, she and I went back into the house to dance. We were waiting for Andrea to leave the boy on the ground and come back to us, so the three of us could be together once again, waving our blue fingernails, intoxicated, dancing before the mirror that reflected no one else.

## Adela's House

I think about Adela every day. And if during the day her memory doesn't visit me—her freckles and her yellow teeth; her blond, too-fine hair; the stump of her shoulder; her little suede boots—she comes to me at night in dreams. My dreams of Adela vary, but there is always the rain and my brother and I, both in our yellow raincoats, standing in front of the empty house and watching the police in the yard as they talk in low voices with our parents.

We made friends with her because she was a suburban princess, spoiled rotten in that enormous English chalet tucked into our gray neighborhood in Lanús. It was like a castle and its inhabitants were lords and the rest of us, in our square cement houses with their straggly gardens, were serfs. We made friends with her because she had the best toys, which her father brought back from his trips to the United States. And because she held the best birthday parties, every January third—just before Día de Reyes and just after New Year's—beside the pool where the water under the siesta sun looked silvered, as if made of wrapping paper. And also because she had a projector and used the white living room walls to watch movies, while the rest of the neighborhood still had black-and-white TVs.

But above all we made friends with her, my brother and I, because Adela had only one arm. Or maybe it would be more precise to say that she was missing an arm. The left one—luckily she wasn't left-handed. It was missing from the shoulder down; she had a small protuberance that moved with a remnant of muscle, but it was useless to her. Adela's parents said she'd been born that way, it was a birth defect. A lot of the other kids were afraid of her, or grossed out by her. They laughed at her, they called her a monster, a Frankenstein, a mutant. They teased her by threatening to sell her to a circus, or that her photo must be in all the medical textbooks.

She didn't care. She didn't even want to use a prosthetic arm. She liked to be looked at and she never hid her stump. If she saw repulsion in someone's eyes, she was capable of rubbing it—her stump—in their face, or sitting very close to the person and caressing his arm with her useless appendage until he was humiliated, almost in tears.

Our mother said Adela had a unique character, that she was brave and strong and set an example, that she was a dear, and had been brought up so well. "She has such good parents," our mother always said. But Adela said her parents were liars. That they lied about her arm. "I wasn't born like this," she'd say. "What happened, then?" we'd ask. And then she told us her version. Her versions, more like it. Sometimes she said her dog had attacked her, a black Doberman named Hell. The dog had gone crazy, a common fate for Dobermans, according to Adela. She said their skulls are too small for their brains, so their heads always hurt and the pain drives them mad; their brains just come unhinged pressed so tight against the bone. She said Hell had attacked her when she was only two years old. She remembered it: the agony, the growling, the sound of his jaws grinding, the blood mixing with the pool water and staining the green grass red. Her father had killed the dog with one shot. He had excellent aim; when the bullet hit the dog, baby Adela was still clenched between Hell's teeth.

My brother didn't believe that version.

"What about the scar, where's the scar?"

She got annoyed.

"It healed really well. You can't see it."

"Impossible. You can always see them."

"I didn't have a scar from the teeth. They had to cut my arm off above the bite."

"Obviously. There would still have to be a scar. They don't just disappear like that."

And as an example he showed her his own scar near his groin from his appendectomy.

"For you, because you had lousy doctors operating on you. I was in the best hospital in Buenos Aires."

"Blah blah blah," my brother said, and he made her cry. He was the only one who could infuriate her. And, even so, they never really fought. He enjoyed her lies. She liked how he challenged her. And I just listened, and that's how we spent the long afternoons after school until my brother and Adela discovered horror movies, and everything changed.

I DON'T KNOW what the first movie was. I wasn't allowed to watch them. My mother said I was too little. "But Adela is the same age as me," I insisted.

"That's her parents' problem if they want to let her. I said no," said my mother, and it was impossible to argue with her.

"But why do you let Pablo?"

"Because he's older than you."

"Because he's a boy!" shouted my father, meddlesome and proud.

"I hate you both!" I screamed, and then I went to bed and cried myself to sleep.

What they couldn't do was stop my brother, Pablo, and Adela from taking pity on me and telling me what happened in the movies. And when they finished relating the movies, they told other stories. I'll never forget those afternoons. When Adela talked, when she concentrated and her dark eyes burned, the house's garden began to fill with shadows, and they ran, they waved to us mockingly. When Adela sat with her back to the picture window, in the living room, I saw them dancing behind her. I didn't tell her. But Adela *knew*. I don't know if my brother did. He was better at hiding things than we were.

He knew how to hide things until the end, right up to his final act, when the only thing left of him was that exposed rib, the crushed skull, and, especially, that arm, his left one, lying between the tracks, so separate from his body and from the train that it didn't seem like the product of the accident—of the suicide. I don't know why I keep calling his suicide an accident. It seemed like someone had carried that arm to the middle of the tracks to display it, like a greeting or a message.

THE TRUTH IS I don't remember which stories were descriptions of movies and which ones Adela or Pablo made up. Ever since the day we went into the house I can't watch horror films. Twenty years later and the fear is still there, and if by chance I watch a scene on TV, I take sleeping pills that night and I feel nauseated for days afterward, remembering how Adela looked sitting there on the sofa in her living room, her stump of an arm, her eyes transfixed, while my brother gazed at her in adoration. Really, I don't remember many of the stories themselves. There was one about a dog possessed by the devil—Adela had a weakness for stories about animals—and another about a man who had chopped up his wife and hidden her limbs in a freezer and the limbs, at night, had come out to chase him, legs and arms and torso and head rolling and dragging themselves around the house, until a dead and vengeful hand strangled the murderer to death. Adela had a weakness, too, for stories about mutilated limbs and amputations. There was another about the ghost of a boy who always appeared in birthday photographs, the terrifying guest no one recognized, his skin gray and a broad grin on his face.

I especially liked the stories about the abandoned house. I even remember the day our obsession with it began. It was my mother's fault. One day after school, my brother and I went with her to the supermarket. She sped up as we walked past the abandoned house that was half a block from the store. We noticed, and we asked her why she was in such a hurry. She laughed. I remember my mother's laugh, and how young she was that sunny afternoon, how her hair smelled of lemon shampoo and she laughed her spearmint gum laughter.

"I'm so silly! . . . Just ignore me. I'm afraid of that house."

She tried to reassure us, to act like an adult, like a mother.

"How come?" asked Pablo.

"No reason, just because it's abandoned."

"So?"

"Don't mind me, sweetheart."

"Come on, tell me!"

"I'm just afraid there's someone hiding in there. A thief, someone like that."

My brother wanted to know more, but my mother didn't have much more to say. The house had been abandoned since before my parents came to the neighborhood, before Pablo was born. She knew that just months before they'd arrived, the owners, an old married couple, had died. "Did they die together?" Pablo wanted to know. "You're getting morbid, sweetheart. I'm going to stop letting you watch those movies. No, they died one after the other. That happens to old couples sometimes; when one dies the other just fades away. And ever since then, their kids have been fighting over the estate."

"What's an estate?" I wanted to know.

"It's the inheritance," said my mother. "They're fighting over who gets to keep the house."

"But the house can't be worth balls," said Pablo, and my mother scolded him for using a bad word.

"What bad word?"

"You know perfectly well. I'm not going to repeat it."

"*Balls* isn't a bad word."

"Pablo, please."

"Fine. But I mean, the house is falling down, Mom."

"What do I know, dear, maybe they want the land. It's the family's problem."

"I bet it's haunted."

"Those movies are a bad influence on you!"

I thought they weren't going to let him watch horror movies anymore, but my mother didn't mention the subject again. And, the next day, my brother told Adela about the house. She was thrilled: a haunted house so close, right there in our neighborhood, barely two blocks away, it was pure joy. "Let's go see it," she said, and the three of us went running out the door, shouting as we ran down the wooden chalet stairs, so pretty (on one side they had stained-glass windows—green, yellow, and red—and the steps were carpeted). Adela ran more slowly than us and leaned a little to one side because of her missing arm, but she ran fast. That afternoon she was wearing a white dress with straps; I remember how when she ran, the left strap fell down over the stump of her arm and she adjusted it automatically, as if brushing a lock of hair from her face.

At first glance there was nothing special about the house, but if you paid a little attention there were some unsettling details. The windows were completely bricked up. "To keep someone from getting in, or something from getting out?" The iron front door was painted dark brown. "It looks like dried blood," said Adela.

"You're such a drama queen," I dared to say. She just smiled at me. She had yellow teeth. Now that did disgust me—not her arm, or lack of one. I don't think she brushed her teeth, and her pale, translucent skin was like a geisha's makeup, making the sickly color stand out even more. She went into the house's tiny front yard. She stood on the walkway that led to the door, turned around, and said:

"Did you notice?"

She didn't wait for our reply.

"It's so weird, how can the grass be this short?"

My brother followed her into the yard, and as if he were

afraid, he also stayed on the stone walkway that led from the sidewalk to the front door.

"It's true," he said. "The grass should be really high. Look, Clara, come here."

I went in. Entering through the rusty gate was horrible. I don't remember it that way just because of what happened later. I'm sure of what I felt then, at that precise moment. It was cold in the yard. And the grass looked burned. Razed. It was yellow and short: not one green weed. Not a single plant. There was an infernal drought in that yard, and it was also winter there. And the house buzzed; it buzzed like a hoarse mosquito, like a fat fly. It vibrated. I didn't run away because I didn't want my brother and Adela to make fun of me, but I felt like fleeing home, to my mother, to tell her: Yes, you're right, that house is an evil mask and it's not thieves behind it, there's a shuddering creature there. Something is hiding there that must not come out.

ADELA AND PABLO talked of nothing but the house. The house was everything. They even asked around in the neighborhood about it. They asked the newsstand vendor and at the social club; they asked Don Justo, who sat in the doorway of his house waiting for sunset; they asked the Galicians at the corner shop, and the vegetable vendor. No one had anything meaningful to tell them. But several people agreed that the house's strange, bricked-up windows and dried-up yard gave them the creeps too, or made them sad, sometimes afraid, especially afraid at night. Many of them remembered the old couple: they were Russian or Lithuanian, very sweet, very quiet. And the children? Some people said they were fighting over the inheritance. Others said they'd never visited their parents, not even when they got sick. No one had seen them, ever. The children, if they existed, were a mystery.

"Someone had to brick up the windows," my brother said to Don Justo.

"Sure they did. But some masons came and did it, not the kids."

"Maybe the masons were the kids."

"I'm sure they weren't. The bricklayers were dark-skinned, and the old couple were blond, translucent. Like you and Adela, like your mom. Polish, they must've been. Something like that."

The idea of going inside the house was my brother's. He suggested it to me first. I told him he was crazy. And he was, he was obsessed. He needed to know what had happened in that house, what was inside. He wanted it with a fervor that was strange to see in an eleven-year-old boy. I don't understand, I could never understand what the house did to him, how it drew him in like that. Because it drew him to it, first. And then he infected Adela.

They sat on the little walkway of yellow and pink paving stones that cut the yard in half. The rusty iron gate was always open, beckoning them in. I went with them, but I stayed outside, on the sidewalk. They stared at the front door as if they thought they could open it with their minds. They spent hours sitting there like that, silent. The people who went by on the sidewalk, our neighbors, didn't pay any attention to them. They didn't think it was strange, or maybe they didn't see them. I didn't dare tell my mother anything.

Or maybe the house wouldn't let me talk. The house didn't want me to save them.

We went on meeting in the living room of Adela's house, but we no longer talked about movies. Now Pablo and Adela—

but especially Adela—told stories about the house. "Where do you get them?" I asked one afternoon, and they glanced at each other in surprise.

"The house tells us the stories. You don't hear it?"

"Poor thing," said Pablo. "She doesn't hear the house's voice."

"It doesn't matter," said Adela. "We'll tell her."

And they told me.

About the old woman, whose eyes had no pupils but who wasn't blind.

About the old man, who burned medical books out by the empty chicken coop, in the backyard.

About the backyard, just as dry and dead as the front, full of little holes like the dens of rats.

About a faucet that never stopped dripping, because the thing that lived in the house needed water.

PABLO HAD TO WORK A LITTLE to convince Adela to go in. It was strange. Now it seemed like she was afraid; they'd switched places. At the decisive moment, she seemed to understand better. My brother insisted. He grabbed her only arm and he even shook her. At school, the kids talked about how Pablo and Adela were boyfriend and girlfriend and they stuck their fingers down their throats like they were throwing up. *Your brother's dating the monster,* they laughed. It didn't bother Pablo and Adela. Me either. My only concern was the house.

They decided we'd go in on the first day of summer. Those were Adela's exact words one afternoon while we talked in the living room at her house.

"The first day of summer, Pablo," she said. "This week."

They wanted me to go with them, and I agreed because I didn't want to leave them. They couldn't go into the dark alone.

We decided to go at night after dinner. We had to sneak out, but getting out of the house in summer wasn't so difficult. In our neighborhood, kids played in the street until late. It's not like that anymore. Now it's a poor and dangerous place, and the neighbors don't go out; they're afraid of being robbed, they're afraid of the teenagers who drink wine on the corners and whose fights sometimes end in gunshots. Adela's chalet was sold and they divided it up into apartments. They built a shed in the garden. It's better now, I think. The shed hides the shadows.

A group of girls was playing jump rope in the middle of the street; when a car went by—very few did—they stopped to let it pass. Farther on more kids were kicking a ball, and where the asphalt was newer, smoother, some teenagers were roller skating. We passed among them unnoticed. Adela was waiting in the dead yard. She was very calm, illuminated. Connected, I think now.

She pointed to the door and I moaned in fear. It was open, just a crack.

"How?" asked Pablo.

"It was like that when I got here."

My brother took off his backpack and opened it. Inside were wrenches, screwdrivers, tire irons—my father's tools that Pablo'd found in a box in the laundry room. Now we wouldn't need them. He was looking for the flashlight.

"We won't need that either," said Adela.

We looked at her, confused. She opened the door all the way, and then we saw that inside the house there was light.

I remember we walked holding hands under that glow that seemed electric, though where there should have been fixtures on the ceiling, there were only old cables sticking out like dry branches. Or maybe the light was like sunlight. Outside it was night and it looked like rain was coming, a powerful summer storm. Inside it was cold and smelled like disinfectant and the light was like a hospital's.

The house didn't seem strange inside. In the small entrance hall was a phone table with a black phone, like the one at our grandparents' house.

*Please don't ring, please don't ring,* I remember praying, repeating it in a low voice with my eyes closed. And it didn't.

The three of us went together into the next room. The house felt bigger than it looked from the outside. And it was buzzing, as if live insects were swarming under the paint on the walls.

Adela moved ahead of us, enthusiastic and unafraid. Every three steps Pablo said, "Wait, wait," and she did, but I don't know if she was hearing clearly. When she turned around to look at us, she seemed lost. There was no recognition in her eyes. She said, "Yes, yes," but I felt as though she wasn't talking to us anymore. Pablo told me later he felt the same way.

The next room, the living room, had dirty, mustard-colored sofas shaded gray by the dust. Against the wall were stacked glass shelves. They were very clean and had lots of little ornaments on them, so small we had to get closer to see what they were. I remember how we stood there all together and our breath fogged up the lowest shelves, the ones we could reach; they went all the way up to the ceiling.

At first I didn't know what I was looking at. They were tiny objects, yellowish white and semicircular. Some were rounded, others sharper. I didn't want to touch them.

"They're fingernails," said Pablo.

I felt like I was going deaf from the buzzing and I started to cry. I hugged Pablo, but I didn't stop looking. On the next shelf, higher up, were teeth. Molars with black lead in the center, like my father's, who'd had them fixed; incisors, like the ones that bothered me when I started wearing a retainer; or sharp canines that reminded me of Roxana, the loudmouthed girl who sat in front of me in school. When I looked up to see what was on the third shelf, the light went out.

Adela screamed in the dark. My heart pounded deafeningly. But I felt my brother, who had his arms around my shoulders and didn't let go. Suddenly I saw a circle of light on the wall: it was the flashlight. I said: "Let's go, let's go." Pablo, though, walked in the opposite direction from the exit. He kept walking farther into the house, and I followed him. I wanted to leave, but not alone.

The flashlight shone onto things that made no sense. A medical book with gleaming pages open on the floor. A mirror hung near the ceiling—who could see a reflection up there? A pile of white clothing. Pablo froze; he moved the flashlight and the light simply didn't show another wall. That room never ended, or its end was too far away for the flashlight to reach it.

"Let's go, let's go," I said again, and I remember I thought about fleeing on my own, about leaving him there and escaping.

"Adela!" Pablo shouted.

We couldn't hear her in the darkness. Where could she be, in that endless room?

"Here."

It was her voice, very quiet, close. She was behind us. We went back. Pablo shined the light toward where her voice was coming from, and then we saw her.

Adela hadn't left the room with the shelves. She was standing next to a door and waving to us with her right hand. Then she turned, opened the door, and closed it behind her. My brother ran, but when he got to the door he couldn't open it. It was locked.

I know what Pablo planned to do: get the tools he'd left outside in the backpack, open the door that had taken Adela. I didn't want to get her out; I only wanted to leave, and I ran out behind him. It was raining outside and the tools were scattered on the yard's dried-out grass; wet, they shone in the night. Someone had taken them out of the backpack. We stayed still for a minute, shaken, surprised, and someone shut the front door from inside.

The house stopped buzzing.

I don't remember how long Pablo spent trying to open it. But at some point he heard me yelling. And he listened.

My parents called the police.

AND EVERY DAY AND ALMOST EVERY NIGHT I return to the rainy gloom of that night. My parents, Adela's parents, the police in the yard. The two of us soaked, wearing our yellow raincoats. More police who came out of the house shaking their heads no. Adela's mother fainting in the rain.

They never found her. Not alive or dead. They asked us to describe the inside of the house. We did. We repeated it. My mother slapped me when I talked about the shelves and the light. "Liar! That house is nothing but rubble inside!" she shouted at me. Adela's mother cried and begged, "Please, where is Adela, where is Adela?"

"In the house," we told her. "She opened a door in the house, she went into a room, and she must still be in there."

The police said there wasn't a single door left in the house. Nor anything that could be considered a room. The house was a shell, they said. All the interior walls had been knocked down.

I remember I heard them say "hell," not "shell." *The house is a hell*, I heard.

We were lying. Or we'd seen something so terrible that we were in shock. They didn't want to believe that we'd even gone into the house. My mother never, ever believed us. Not even after the police searched the entire neighborhood, raiding every house. The case was on TV, and they let us watch the news. They let us read the magazines that talked about the disappearance. Adela's mother came to see us several times and she always said: "Let's see if you'll tell me the truth, kids, let's see if you remember . . ."

We would tell her everything again, and she'd leave in tears. My brother cried, too. "I convinced her, I made her go in," he said.

One night, my father woke up and heard someone trying to open the door. He got out of bed and crept downstairs, expecting to find a burglar. Instead he found Pablo struggling with the key in the lock—that door was always tricky. He was carrying tools and a flashlight in his backpack. I heard them yelling at each other for hours, and I remember my brother saying please, he wanted to move away, and that if he didn't move away he was going to go crazy.

We moved. My brother still went crazy. He killed himself at twenty-two. I was the one who identified his ruined body. I had no choice—my parents were at the beach on vacation when he threw himself under the train, far away from our house, near the Beccar station. He didn't leave a note. He'd told me his dreams were always about Adela. In his dreams, our friend didn't have fingernails or teeth; she was bleeding from the mouth, her hands bled.

Since Pablo killed himself, I've started going back to the house. I go into the yard, which is still burned and yellow. I look in through its windows, open like black eyes; the police knocked out the bricks that covered them fifteen years ago and they stayed like that, open. Inside, when the sun shines in, you can see beams and the roof full of holes and the ground littered with garbage. The neighborhood kids know what happened there. They've spray-painted Adela's name on the floor. On the walls outside, too. *Where is Adela?* says one scrawled message. Another, smaller and written in marker, repeats an urban legend: you have to say *Adela* three times at midnight in front of a mirror, holding a candle in your hand. Then you'll see the reflection of what she saw, the thing that took her.

My brother had also visited the house and seen those instructions, and one night he performed the ritual. He didn't see anything. He smashed the bathroom mirror with his fist and we had to take him to the hospital to get stitches.

I can't get up the courage to go inside. There's a message over the door that keeps me out. *Here lives Adela. Beware!* it says. I'm sure some kid from the neighborhood wrote it as a joke or on a dare. But I know it's true. It's her house. And I'm still not ready to visit.

## An Invocation of the Big-Eared Runt

The first time he appeared to Pablo was on the bus during the nine-thirty tour. It happened during a pause in his narration while they rode from the restaurant that had belonged to Emilia Basil (dismemberer) to the building where Yiya Murano (poisoner) had lived. Of all the tours of Buenos Aires the company he worked for offered, the murder tour was the most popular. It ran four times a week: twice by bus and twice on foot, two times in English and two times in Spanish. Pablo knew that when the company appointed him as a guide on the murder tour, they were giving him a promotion, even though the salary was the same (he knew that if he did well, sooner or later the salary would go up, too). He'd been quite happy about the change: before, he'd been leading the Art Nouveau of Avenida de Mayo tour, which was interesting at first but got boring after a while.

He had studied the tour's ten crimes in detail so he could narrate them well, with humor and suspense, and he'd never felt scared—they didn't affect him at all. That's why, when he saw the apparition, he felt more surprise than terror. It was definitely him, no doubt about it. He was unmistakable: the large, damp eyes that looked full of tenderness but were really dark wells of idiocy. The drab sweater on his short body, his puny shoulders, and in his hands the thin rope he'd used to demonstrate to the police, emotionless all the while, how he had tied up and strangled his victims. And then there were his enormous ears, pointed and affable. His name was Cayetano Santos Godino, but his nickname was El Petiso Orejudo: the Big-Eared Runt. He was the most famous criminal on the tour, maybe the most famous in Argentine police record. A murderer of children and small animals. A murderer who didn't know how to read or add, who couldn't tell you the days of the week, and who kept a box full of dead birds under his bed.

But it was impossible for him to be there, where Pablo saw him standing. The Runt had died in 1944 at the Ushuaia penitentiary in Tierra del Fuego, a thousand miles away, down at the end of the world. What could he possibly be doing now, in the spring of 2014, a ghost passenger on a bus touring the scenes of his crimes? Pablo was positive it was him. The apparition was identical to the many photos that had survived. Plus, it was bright enough to see him well: the bus's lights were on. He was standing almost at the end of the aisle, demonstrating with his rope and looking at the guide—at him, Pablo—somewhat indifferently but undeniably.

Pablo had been telling the Runt's story for a while (two weeks now) and he liked it a lot. The Big-Eared Runt had stalked a Buenos Aires so distant and so different from today's that it was hard to be disturbed by the thought of such a character. And yet something must have left a deep impression on Pablo, because the Runt had appeared only to him. No one else could see the apparition—the passengers were talking animatedly and they looked right through him, they didn't notice him.

Pablo shook his head, shut his eyes tightly, and when he opened them, the figure of the murderer with his rope had disappeared. *Am I going crazy?* he thought, and he comforted himself with some pseudo psychology: surely he was seeing the Runt because he and his wife had just had a baby, and children were Godino's only victims. Small children. On his tour, Pablo explained where, according to the experts of the time, the Runt's predilection had come from: the Godinos' first son, the Runt's older brother, had died at ten months old in Calabria, Italy, before the family immigrated to Argentina. The memory of that dead baby had obsessed him. In many of his crimes—and his attempted crimes, which were much more numerous—the Runt imitated the burial ceremony. He'd told the detectives who interrogated him after he was caught: "No one comes back from the dead. My brother never came back. He's just rotting underground."

Pablo would tell the story of the Runt's first simulated burial at one of the tour's stops: the intersection of Calle Loria and San Carlos, where the Runt had attacked Ana Neri, eighteen months old, the daughter of a neighbor in the Liniers tenement. The building no longer existed, but the site where it had once stood was a stop on the tour, with a short contextualization to explain to the tourists what living conditions had been like for those recently arrived immigrants fleeing poverty in Europe: they were stuffed into rented rooms that were damp, dirty, noisy, unventilated dens of promiscuity. It was the ideal environment for the Runt's crimes, because the squalor and chaos ended up driving everyone out to the street. Living in those rooms was so unbearable that people spent all their time on the sidewalks, especially the children, who roamed unchecked from a very early age.

Ana Neri. The Runt brought her to the empty lot, hit her with a rock, and once the girl was unconscious he tried to bury her. A policeman chanced upon him before he could finish, and the Runt quickly improvised an alibi: he said he'd been trying to help the child after someone else had attacked her. The policeman believed him, possibly because the Big-Eared Runt was a child too: he was only nine years old.

It took Ana six months to recover.

And that wasn't the only attack involving a simulated burial: in September 1908, shortly after he dropped out of school—and after he started having fits of what seemed like epilepsy, though they never really figured out what caused the Runt's convulsions—he brought another child, Severino González, to a vacant lot across from the Sacred Heart school. There was a small horse corral on the lot. The Runt submerged the boy in the animals' water trough and then tried to cover it with a wooden lid. A more sophisticated simulacrum: an imitation coffin. Once again, a policeman passing by put a stop to the crime, and once again the Runt lied and said that he was actually helping the boy. But that month the Runt couldn't control himself. On September 15 he attacked a fifteen-month-old baby, Julio Botte. He found him in the doorway of his house at 632 Colombres. He burned one of the boy's eyelids with a cigarette he was smoking. Two months later, the Runt's parents couldn't bear his presence or his actions anymore, and they turned him over to the police themselves. In December he was sent to the juvenile detention center in Marcos Paz. He learned to write a little while he was there, but he was most notorious for throwing cats and boots into steaming pots in the kitchen when the cooks weren't looking. The Runt served three years in the Marcos Paz reformatory. When he was released, his desire to kill was stronger than ever, and soon he would achieve his first, longed-for murder.

Pablo always ended the section on the Runt with the police

interrogation after his arrest. It seemed to leave quite an impression on the tourists. He would read from a transcript to make it seem more immediate. The night the Runt appeared on the bus, Pablo felt somewhat uncomfortable repeating the killer's own words with him standing there, but he decided to proceed as usual. The Runt just looked at him and played with his rope.

*—Isn't your conscience troubled by the crimes you have committed?*

*—I don't understand what you are asking me.*

*—You don't know what a conscience is?*

*—No, sir.*

*—Do you feel sadness or regret about the deaths of the children you killed?*

*—No, sir.*

*—Do you think you have the right to kill children?*

*—I'm not the only one. Others do it too.*

*—Why did you kill the children?*

*—Because I liked it.*

This last response brought on general discomfort among the passengers. They usually seemed happy when the tour moved on to the more understandable Yiya Murano, who poisoned her best friends because they owed her money. A murderer born of ambition. Easy to wrap your head around. The Runt, on the other hand, made everyone uneasy.

That night, when he got home, Pablo didn't tell his wife that he had seen the Runt's ghost. He hadn't told his coworkers either, but that was only natural: he didn't want any problems at work. It bothered him, though, that he couldn't talk to his wife about the vision. Two years ago he would have told her. Two years ago, back when they could still tell each other anything without fear, without mistrust. It was only one of so many things that had changed since the baby had been born.

His name was Joaquín and he was six months old, but Pablo still called him "the baby." He loved him—at least, he thought he did—but the baby didn't pay much attention to him. He still clung to his mother, and she didn't help, she did not help at all. She had turned into a different person. Fearful, suspicious, obsessive. Pablo sometimes wondered if she might be suffering from postpartum depression. Other times he just got sulky and thought back to the years before the baby with nostalgia and a little—well, more than a little—anger.

Everything was different now. For example, she didn't listen to him anymore. She pretended to, she smiled and nodded, but she was thinking about buying carrots and squash for the baby, or about whether the skin of the baby's hips was irritated from the disposable diaper or from some spreading disease. She didn't listen to him, and she didn't want to have sex with him, because she was sore from the episiotomy that just wouldn't scar over. And to top it off, the baby slept with them in the conjugal bed. There was a bedroom waiting for him, but she couldn't bring herself to let him sleep alone; she was afraid of sudden infant death syndrome. Pablo had had to listen to her talk about that white death for hours while he tried in vain to calm her—she who had never been afraid before, who once upon a time had gone with him to scale high peaks and sleep in mountain huts while the snow fell outside. She who'd taken mushrooms with him, hallucinating for a whole weekend, that same woman now cried over a death that had not come and that maybe never would.

Pablo couldn't remember why having a baby had even

seemed like a good idea. Now she never talked about anything else—no more gossiping about neighbors, no more discussing movies, family scandals, work, politics, food, travel. Now she only talked about the baby and pretended to listen when other subjects arose. The only thing she seemed to register, as if it woke her up from a trance, was the name of the Big-Eared Runt. As if her mind lit up with the vision of the idiot assassin's eyes or as if she knew those thin fingers that held the rope. She said Pablo was obsessed with the Runt. He didn't think that was true. It was just that the other murderers on the Buenos Aires horror tour were all boring. The city didn't have any great murderers if you didn't count the dictators—not included in the tour for reasons of political correctness. Some of the murderers he talked about had committed crimes that were atrocious, but they still conformed well to any catalog of pathological violence. The Runt was different. He was strange. He had no motive besides desire, and he seemed like some kind of metaphor, the dark side of proud turn-of-the-century Argentina. He was a foretaste of evils to come, a warning that there was much more to the country than palaces and estates; he was a slap in the face to the provincialism of the Argentine elites who worshipped Europe and believed only good things could come from the magnificent and yearned-for old country. The most beautiful part was that the Runt didn't have the slightest awareness of any of this. He just *enjoyed* attacking children and lighting fires—because he was a pyromaniac, too. He liked to see the flames and watch the firefighters as they worked. "Especially," he told one of the interrogators later, "when they fall in the fire."

It was a story about fire that really made his wife fly off the handle: she'd gotten up from the table screaming at him that he was never to talk about the Runt around her again, ever, not for any reason. She had shouted it while clutching the baby like she was afraid the Runt would appear and attack him right there. Then she'd locked herself in the bedroom and left Pablo to eat alone. Under his breath, he told her to go to hell.

The story really was impressive. No cause for such a fuss, he thought, but it was pretty brutal. It had happened on March 7, 1912. A five-year-old girl, Reina Bonita Vaínikoff, daughter of Latvian-Jewish immigrants, was looking in the window of a shoe store near her house on Avenida Entre Ríos. The girl was wearing a white dress. The Runt approached her while she was absorbed in the sight of the shoes. He was holding a lit match in his hand. He held the flame to her dress and it caught fire. The girl's grandfather saw her from across the street as she was engulfed in flames. The grandfather ran desperately to reach her, but he never even got near the girl: mad with fear, he hadn't noticed the traffic. A car ran over him and he died. Very strange when you consider the slow speed of cars in those years.

Reina Bonita died too, but only after sixteen days of agonizing pain.

Poor Reina Bonita's murder wasn't Pablo's favorite crime. He liked—because that was the word, what can you do?—the murder of Jesualdo Giordano, three years old. Without a doubt, that one inspired the most horror in the tourists, and maybe that's why he liked it: maybe he found it pleasant to tell the story and wait for the reaction of his audience—they were always shocked. Plus, it was the crime they'd caught the Runt for, because he committed a fatal error.

As was his habit by now, the Runt brought Jesualdo to an empty lot. He strangled him by winding the rope thirteen times around his neck. The boy fought back with all his strength, he cried and screamed. The Runt told the police that he'd struggled to keep the boy quiet because he didn't want to be interrupted as he'd been on other occasions: "I grabbed that kid with my teeth right here, near his mouth, and I shook him the way dogs do with cats." That image distressed the tourists, who squirmed in their seats and murmured "my God" under their breath. But they never asked him to stop the story. Once he'd strangled Jesualdo to death, the Runt covered him with sheet metal and went out to the street. But something kept tormenting him, an idea burning in his mind. So after a while he went back to the scene of the crime. He was holding a nail. He drove it into the boy's skull, though Jesualdo was already dead.

He committed his fatal error the next day. Who knows why, but he attended the wake of the boy he had killed. Later on he would say that he wanted to see if the nail was still in the head. He confessed this desire when they brought him in to witness the autopsy, after the dead boy's father had pointed the finger at the Runt. When the Runt saw the cadaver, he did something very strange: he covered his nose and spat as if he were disgusted, though the body had not yet begun to decompose. For some reason—the police records of the time don't explain it—the medical examiners made him remove his clothes, and the Runt had an enormous erection. He had just turned sixteen.

Pablo couldn't tell that story to his wife. Once, he'd tried to tell her about how the tourists reacted to the Runt's final crime, but before he could even begin the story he realized that she wasn't listening to him. Instead, she started complaining, demanding they move to a bigger house when the baby was older. She didn't want him to grow up in an apartment. She wanted a yard, a pool, a game room, and all in a peaceful neighborhood where the boy could play in the street. She knew perfectly well that such a place barely existed in a city the size and intensity of Buenos Aires, and moving to a rich and tranquil suburb was far beyond their means. When she finished listing her desires for the future, she asked him to get a new job. "I won't do that," he said. "My degree is in tourism, things are going well for me. I'm not going to quit—it's fun, the hours are good, and I'm learning."

"The salary is pitiful."

"No, it's not pitiful." Pablo was getting angry. As he saw it he was earning good money, enough to decently maintain his family. Who was this woman, this stranger? Once upon a time she had sworn that as long as she was with him, she could live in a motel, in the street, under a tree. It was all the baby's fault. The baby had changed her completely. And why? He was a charmless kid, boring, all he ever did was sleep, and when he was awake he cried almost nonstop. "Why don't *you* go to work if you want more money?" Pablo asked his wife. At that she seemed to bristle, and she started shouting like she'd gone crazy. She screamed that *she* had to take care of the baby—what was he thinking, that she could just dump him with a babysitter, or with his crazy grandmother? *My mother isn't crazy*, thought Pablo, and to avoid another shouting match he went out to the sidewalk to smoke. That was another thing: since the baby had been born, she wouldn't let him smoke in his own apartment.

The day after the argument, the Runt came back to the bus. This time he was closer, almost right next to the driver, who clearly couldn't see him. Pablo didn't feel any different, just a little uneasy; he was afraid one of the tourists would be able to see the ghostly Runt and would cause chaos on the bus.

When the Runt appeared, holding his rope, they were almost at the end of the tour, at the house on Calle Pavón. That was where one of the Runt's oldest victims had been found, after one of his strangest attacks. Arturo Laurora, thirteen years old, had been strangled with his own shirt; his body was found inside the abandoned house. He wasn't wearing pants and his buttocks were bruised, but he hadn't been raped. While Pablo told this story, the ghost of the Runt, standing beside him, appeared and disappeared, trembled, faded, as if he were made of smoke or fog.

For the first time in many nights someone had a question. Pablo smiled at the curious man with all the insincerity he could muster. Pablo thought the tourist must be Caribbean, judging by the way he pronounced the word *clavo*, nail. The man wanted to know if the Runt had driven a nail into any of his other victims' heads. "No," replied Pablo. "We only know of the one."

"It's very strange," said the man, and he ventured that if the Runt's criminal career had been longer, maybe the nail would have become his trademark, his signature. "Maybe so," Pablo answered politely as he watched the spectral Runt disappear completely. "But I guess we'll never know, huh?" The Caribbean man scratched his chin.

Pablo went back to his house thinking about the nail, and then about a math teacher he'd had in school. When he got a problem right she'd say, "Pablito! You hit the nail on the head." Then he thought about a tongue twister his mother had taught him when he was little: *Pablito clavó un clavito. / ¿Qué clavito clavó Pablito? / Un clavito chiquitito.* He opened the apartment door to find the tableau that had become so common in recent months: the television on, a plate with *Ben 10* cartoons on it smeared with the remains of pureed squash, a half-empty bottle, and his bedroom light turned on. He looked in. His wife and son were sleeping on the bed, together.

Pablo walked to the room that he himself had decorated

for his son before he'd been born. It was so empty he felt cold. The inert crib was dark. It was like a dead child's room kept untouched by a family in mourning. Pablo wondered what would happen if the boy died, as his wife seemed to fear. He knew the answer.

He leaned against the empty wall where months ago, before the birth, before his wife turned into a different person, he'd planned to hang a mobile: a universe that would spin over the baby's crib and keep him entertained during the night. The moon, the sun, Jupiter, Mars, and Saturn, the planets and satellites and stars shining in the darkness. But he had never hung it because his wife didn't want the baby to sleep in his crib and there was no way of changing her mind. He touched the wall and he found the nail still there, waiting. He yanked it out with one tug and put it in his pocket. He thought it would make a great prop, adding to the dramatic effect of his story about the Runt. He would take it from his pocket right when he was telling about Jesualdo Giordano's murder, at just the right moment, when the Runt came back and drove the nail into the dead boy's head. Maybe some naïve tourist would even believe it was the very same nail, perfectly preserved a hundred years after the crime. He smiled as he imagined his small triumph, and he decided he'd lie down right there on the living room sofa, far from his wife and his son, the nail still clutched in his hand.

# Spiderweb

It's harder to breathe in the humid north, up there so close to Brazil and Paraguay, the rushing river guarded by mosquito sentinels and a sky that can turn from limpid blue to stormy black in minutes. You start to struggle right away when you arrive, as if a brutal arm were wound around your waist and squeezing. Everything is slower; during siesta the bicycles only rarely go by along the empty street, the ice cream shops seem abandoned in spite of the ceiling fans that spin for no one, and the *chicharras* shriek hysterically in their hiding places. I've never seen a *chicharra*. My aunt says they're horrible creatures, spectacular flies with pulsating green wings and smooth, black eyes that seem to look right at you. I don't like the word *chicharra*; I wish they were always called cicadas, which is only used when they're in the larval stage. If they were called cicadas, their summer noise would remind me of the violet flowers of the jacaranda trees along the Paraná, or the white stone mansions with their staircases and their willows. But as it is, as *chicharras*, they make me remember the heat, the rotting meat, the blackouts, the drunks who stare with bloodshot eyes from their benches in the park.

That February I went to visit my aunt and uncle in Corrientes because I was tired of their reproaches: "You got married and we haven't even met your husband, how is that possible, you're hiding him from us."

"No," I laughed over the phone, "how could I be hiding him, I'd love for you to meet him, we'll come soon."

But they were right: I was hiding him.

My aunt and uncle were the custodians of the memory of my mother, their favorite sister, killed in a stupid accident when I was seventeen. During the first months of mourning they offered to have me come live with them in the north. I said no. They came to visit me often. They gave me money, called me every day. My cousins stayed to keep me company on weekends. But I still felt abandoned, and because of that solitude I fell in love too quickly, I got married impetuously, and now I was living with Juan Martín, who irritated and bored me.

I decided to bring him to meet my aunt and uncle to see if other eyes could transform him in mine. One meal on the wide porch of their big house was enough to dispel that hope: Juan Martín squealed when a spider brushed his leg ("If they don't have a pink cross, don't worry," my uncle Carlos told him, a cigarette between his lips. "Those are the only poisonous ones."), drank too much beer, spoke with zero modesty about how well business was going, and commented several times on the "underdevelopment" that he saw in the province.

After we ate he sat with my uncle Carlos, drinking whiskey, and I helped my aunt in the kitchen.

"Well, child, it could be worse," she told me when I started to cry. "He could be like Walter, who raised his hand to me."

Yes, I nodded. Juan Martín wasn't violent; he wasn't even jealous. But he repelled me. How many years was I going to spend like that, disgusted when I heard his voice, pained when we had sex, silent when he confided his plans to have a child and renovate the house? I wiped away my tears with hands covered in soap suds; they burned my eyes and I cried even harder. My aunt pushed my head under the faucet and let the water wash my eyes out for ten minutes. That's how we were when Natalia came in. Natalia was my aunt's oldest daughter and my favorite cousin. Natalia, tanned as always, wearing a very loose white dress, her hair long, dark, and disheveled. I saw her through the fog of my irritated eyes, which I couldn't stop blinking; she was carrying a flowerpot and smoking. Everyone smokes in Corrientes. If anyone ever dared to hint that it wasn't healthy, they'd stand looking at the heretic, confused, and then give a little laugh.

Natalia placed the flowerpot on the kitchen table, told my aunt, her mother, that she had planted the azalea, and she greeted me with a kiss on the head. My husband didn't like Natalia. He didn't find her physically attractive, which was practically insane on his part—I had never seen a woman as beautiful as her. But on top of that, he looked down on her because Natalia read cards, knew home remedies, and worst of all, communicated with spirits. "Your cousin is ignorant," Juan Martín told me, and I hated him. I even thought about calling Natalia and asking her to give me a recipe for one of her potions, maybe a poison. But I let it go, like I let every petty little thing pass while a white stone grew in my stomach that left very little room for air or food.

"Tomorrow I'm going to Asunción," Natalia told me. "I need to buy some *ñandutí* cloth."

To earn money, Natalia had a small business selling crafts in the city's main street, and she was famous for her exquisite taste in choosing the finest *ñandutí*, the traditional Paraguayan lace that the women weave on a frame, spiderwebs of delicate, colorful thread. In the back part of her shop she had a small table where she read cards, Spanish or tarot, according to the customer's preference. They say she was very good. I couldn't say for sure because I'd never wanted her to read cards for me.

"Why don't you come with me? We can take your husband. Has he been to Asunción?"

"No—as if."

Natalia flip-flopped her way to the patio and greeted Uncle Carlos and Juan Martín with kisses on the cheek. She poured a whiskey with a lot of ice and stretched her toes. I emerged from the kitchen with swollen eyes and Juan Martín asked how I could be so dumb. "If you'd injured your corneas we'd have to rush back to Buenos Aires by plane."

"Why?" asked Natalia, and she shook the ice in her glass so it sounded like little bells in the afternoon heat. "The hospital here is very good."

"It doesn't compare."

"Well, aren't you a citified little prick." And after she said that, she invited him to Asunción. "I'm driving," she told him. "You can buy stuff if you have money, everything's cheap. It's three hundred kilometers; we can go and come back the same day if we leave early."

He accepted. Then he went to take a nap and didn't even suggest I join him. I was grateful. I stayed with my cousin out on the hot porch, she with her whiskey, me with a cold beer. I couldn't drink anything stronger. She told me about her new boyfriend, the son of the owner of the province's largest supermarket chain. She always had rich boyfriends. This one mattered to her as little as the others, emotionally speaking, but she was interested in him because he had a plane. He'd taken her up in it the week before. "Beautiful," she told me, "except it shakes a little. The smaller the plane the more it shakes."

"I didn't know that," I told her.

"Me either. Aren't we dumb, cousin, because it makes sense.

"Something terrifying happened to me while I was up there," she went on. "We were flying over fields to the north, and suddenly I saw a very big fire. A house was burning, bright orange flames and a black cloud of smoke, and you could see the house collapsing in on itself. I stared and stared at the fire until he turned the plane and I lost sight of it. But ten minutes later we passed over the spot again and the fire had disappeared."

"You must have gotten the place wrong. It's not like you're up in planes all the time and you can recognize the terrain from above."

"You don't understand, there was a patch of burned earth and the ruins of the house."

"It went out, then."

"How? Did the firefighters get there in five minutes? We're talking wilderness here, babe, and the flames were really high when I saw them, and it wasn't raining or anything! It could never have been put out in ten minutes."

"Did you tell your boyfriend?"

"Sure, but he says I'm crazy, he never saw any fire."

Our eyes met. I almost always believed her. Once, Natalia had stopped me from going into my grandmother's room because she was in there, smoking. Our grandmother had been dead for ten years. I listened to her: I didn't go in, but I smelled the penetrating odor of the Havana cigarillos that were her favorites, though there was no smoke in the air.

"You have to find out, then, ask around."

"I don't want to."

"Why not?"

"Because I don't know if the fire already happened, or if it's going to happen."

It was still dark when we left, five in the morning. Juan Martín almost let us go alone, because according to him he'd barely slept at all, thanks to the heat and the power outage that had left him without a fan. But lying in the darkness, awake, I had listened to him snoring and talking in his sleep. He lied and complained, and every day was the same as the one before. Natalia had a Renault 12, the most common car there was during the eighties. When the sun started to come out over Route 11, I saw that, trapped under its windshield wipers, were the bodies of many dead damselflies. A lot of people get them confused them with dragonflies, but the damselfly is different, though they're in the same family. They're less graceful, their horrible eyes are farther apart, and the body, that straight and vaguely phallic body, is longer. They're lazier, too. I was always afraid of both of them and I never understood when they came into fashion years later with teenagers, who tattooed themselves with sentimental designs, dolphins and butterflies, and but also those horrible dragonflies with their blind eyes. Some people call them *aguaciles*—from the word *agua*—because bands of them tend to show up before it rains, when it's really hot. That word makes me think of *alguacil*—sheriff—and I think a lot of people call the insect that, as if it were the police of the air.

The road to Asunción is boring and monotonous; at times it's palm trees with marshlands, other times jungle, and much more rarely a small city or a village. Juan Martín slept in the backseat, and sometimes I looked at him in the rearview mirror: he was attractive in his privileged way, with his elegant haircut and his polo shirt with the Lacoste crocodile. Natalia was smoking her long Benson & Hedges, but we didn't talk because she was driving very fast and the noise would have forced us to shout. I wanted to tell her more things about my marriage. Like how Juan Martín constantly chastised me. If I took too long to serve the table I was useless, just "standing there doing nothing, as always." If I took too long to choose something, I was wasting his time—he was always so decisive and detached. If I deliberated for ten minutes about what restaurant to go to, it meant a night of his sighing and contrary replies. I always apologized so we wouldn't fight, so things wouldn't get worse. I never told him all the things that bothered me about him, like how he belched after eating, how he never cleaned the bathroom even though I begged him to, how he was always complaining about the quality of things, how when I asked him for a little humor he always said it was too late for that, he'd already lost his patience. But I kept quiet. When we stopped for lunch I split a polenta with my cousin while Juan Martín ate the same steak with salad he ate every day. He never wanted anything else. At most he'd try cutlets or shepherd's pie. And pizza, but only on weekends.

He was boring and I was stupid. I felt like asking one of the truckers to run me over and leave me gutted on the road, split open like the dogs I saw occasionally lying dead on the asphalt. Some of them had been pregnant, too heavy to run fast and escape the murderous wheels, and their puppies lay agonizing around them.

When we were less than an hour from the border with Paraguay, we got our passports ready. The immigration officials were tall, dark soldiers. One of them was drunk. They let us through without paying much attention to us, though they checked out our asses and made crude comments, laughing. Their attitude was predictable and relatively respectful; they were there to instill fear, to dissuade any challenge. Juan Martín said—once we were far from the checkpoint—that we had to file a complaint.

"And just who are you going to complain to, buddy, when those guys are the government?" Natalia asked him, and I, who knew her well, heard something more than teasing in her voice; it held contempt. Then she looked at me incredulously. But none of us said anything more. Natalia, who knew her way around Asunción, got us straight to Market 4 and left the car locked two blocks away. We walked, accosted by watch and tablecloth vendors, begging children, a mother and her wheelchair-bound daughter—all under the watchful eyes of the soldiers with their greenish-brown uniforms and their enormous guns that looked ancient, out-of-date, little-used.

The heat and the smell of the market were a physical blow, and I came to a stop near an orange stand. In Paraguay they call them *toronjas* instead of *naranjas*, and the fruits have a kind of deformed belly button and a bland flavor. The fruit at the market stand was circled by those little flies that I hate, not because they disgust me but simply because I don't know how to kill them. They were like little flying fragments of darkness because you had to have them very close to your eyes to see wings or legs or any bug-like characteristics. I didn't buy any oranges even though the vendor lowered her price again and again: three *guaraníes*, two *guaraníes*, one *guaraní*. The porters ran down aisles pushing trolleys with boxes, some full of fruit, others filled with televisions and dual-cassette players, still others with clothes. Juan Martín was silent, and Natalia walked decisively ahead in her white dress and flat leather sandals. She had tied her hair back in the heat, and her ponytail swayed from side to side as if the wind blew only for her.

"This is all contraband," Juan Martín said suddenly, loud enough for some stallholders and wandering vendors to turn and look at him. I stopped short and grabbed his arm. "Don't talk like that," I said into his ear.

"They're all criminals, where have you brought me, this is your family?" The nausea mixed with the tears when I told him that we were going to talk later, that he should shut up now, that yes, there were probably some criminals there and they were going to kill us if he kept provoking them. I looked him up and down: his boat shoes, the sweat stains in his armpits, the sunglasses pushed up over his hair. I didn't love him anymore, I didn't desire him, and I would have handed him right over to Stroessner's soldiers and let them do as they pleased.

I hurried to catch up with Natalia, who was already at the stand of the woman who sold *ñandutí*. A younger woman was weaving the cloth with vibrant colors. It was the only place in that endless and noisy market where there was something like calm. People stopped and asked about prices and the woman answered in a quiet voice, but they heard her in spite of the radios, the *chamamé* music, even a man who was playing the harp for the few tourists who had braved the trip into Asunción that hot morning to buy on the cheap. Natalia took her time. She debated between several tablecloths and finally chose five sets with their napkins; my favorites were the white one with details of every color around the edges and in the center—violet, blue, turquoise, green, red, orange, yellow—and another much more elegant one that used only a palette of browns, from beige to mahogany. She bought the five sets, some thirty table runners, and many details to sew onto dresses and shirts, especially on *guayaberas* that she bought at another stand farther on. To find it, we had to move deeper into the market. I followed her and didn't even check to see whether Juan Martín was following me. I thought about why *ñandutí* was called "spiderweb" cloth. It must be because of the weaving technique, because really the end result seemed much more like a peacock's tail: the feathers with their eyes, beautiful but disturbing. Many eyes arrayed above the animal, which walks so heavily—a beautiful animal, but one that always seems tired.

"Wouldn't you like a *guayabera* for yourself, Martín?" Natalia called him Martín; she didn't use his full name. Juan Martín was uncomfortable, but he tried to smile. I knew that expression, it was his tough guy face and it said *I'm doing all I can,* so that later, when everything went to hell once we got back, he could rub it in my face, smear it all over my mouth: *I tried but you didn't help at all, you never help.* He bought the *guayabera* but didn't want to try it on. "I have to wash it first," he told me reproachfully, as if the shirt could be poisoned. He carried one of Natalia's plastic bags for her—they weren't even that heavy, it was only cloth—and he said, "Please, can we get out of this hellhole?" Since the exit wasn't marked he had no choice but to follow us. To follow Natalia, really, and I saw the disgust and resentment in his eyes.

My cousin linked arms with me and pretended to admire a bracelet of silver and lapis lazuli that Juan Martín had given me on our honeymoon in Valparaíso.

"We all make mistakes," she told me. "The important thing is to fix them."

"And how does this get fixed?"

"Babe, death is the only problem without a solution."

JUAN MARTÍN DIDN'T like the trip from the market to the bay; he thought the city looked dirty and poor. He didn't like the presidential palace and later, at the beach along the river, he started practically shouting at us: how could we be so anesthetized, didn't we see the potbellied kids eating watermelon under the beating sun, and right in front of the house of government, please, what a shitty country. We didn't want to argue with him. The city *was* poor, and in the heat it smelled like garbage. But he wasn't disgusted with Asunción, he was mad at us. I didn't even feel like crying anymore. To placate him we looked for a restaurant around there, where the ministries were, the private schools, the embassies and hotels: Paraguay's rich. We quickly came to the Munich, on Calle Presidente Franco. "Is it named after Franco, the dictator?" asked Juan Martín, but it was a rhetorical question. On the restaurant patio there was an enormous effigy of Saint Rita and the tables were empty, except the one in the middle, where three soldiers sat. We chose a table far from them so they wouldn't overhear Juan Martín, and also because it is always preferable to sit far away from soldiers in Asunción. The walls were colonial, the square of sky above us was totally clear, but there was shade on the patio in spite of the heat. We ordered Paraguayan corn bread, and Juan Martín, a sandwich. The soldiers, drunk on beer—there were several empty bottles on the table and under their chairs—first told the waitress she was beautiful, and then one of them touched her ass, and it was like a movie in poor taste, a bad joke: the man with his uniform jacket unbuttoned over his distended belly, a toothpick between his teeth, the grotesque laughter, and the girl who tried to brush them off by asking, "Can I get you anything else?" But she didn't dare insult them because they had their guns at their waists, and others were leaning against the flower bed behind them.

Juan Martín got up and I could just imagine what was going to happen next. He was going to yell at them to leave her alone; he was going to play the hero, and then they would arrest all three of us. They would rape Natalia and me in the dictator's dungeons, day and night, and they would torture me with electric shocks on my pubic hair that was as blond as the hair on my head, and they would drool while they said *fucking little gringa, fucking Argentine*, and maybe they would kill Natalia quickly, for being dark, for being a witch, for being insolent. And all because he needed to be a hero and prove God only knows what. Anyway, he would have it easy because they killed men with a bullet through the back of the skull, and done. They weren't fags, the Paraguayan soldiers, of course they weren't.

Natalia stopped him.

"But don't you see what they're doing? They're going to rape her."

"I see everything," said Natalia, "but we can't do anything. We're leaving now." Natalia left money on the table and dragged Juan Martín toward the car. The soldiers didn't even notice us, they were so focused on tormenting the girl. In the car, Juan Martín told us everything he thought about our cowardice and how sick and ashamed we made him. It was six in the afternoon. We had spent many hours shopping at the market and trying to sightsee on the oceanfront and downtown, putting up with my husband's whining. Natalia wanted to get back early so we could have dinner in Corrientes, so she started the car and we headed out of Asunción as the sun was turning red and the fruit vendors were sitting down to drink something cool under their umbrellas.

THE CAR STALLED ON THE WAY BACK, somewhere in Formosa. It started bucking like a rebellious horse and then it stopped; when Natalia tried to start it again, I recognized the impotent sound of the motor, suffocated and exhausted. If it was going to turn over at all, it would be a while. The darkness was complete; along that stretch of the road there was no illumination. But the worst thing was the silence, barely cut by some nocturnal bird, by slidings through the plants—it was jungle there, thick vegetation—or by the occasional truck that sounded very far away, and that wasn't going to come and save us.

"Why don't you take a look under the hood?" I said to my husband. I'd already been fairly annoyed when he hadn't offered to drive on the way back; he hadn't even asked my cousin if she was tired. I didn't know how to drive. Why was I so useless? Had I been so spoiled by my dead mother? Had it occurred to no one that I would ever have to solve problems by myself? Had I married this imbecile because I didn't know what to do or how to work? In the darkness, in among the barely visible vegetation, the fireflies shone. I hate when people call them lightning bugs; *firefly* is a beautiful word. Once, I caught a bunch of them in an empty mayonnaise jar, and I realized how ugly they really are, like cockroaches with wings. But they've been blessed with the purest possible justice. Still and grounded, they look like a pest, but when they fly and light up, they are the closest thing to magic, a portent of beauty and goodness.

Juan Martín asked for a flashlight and went outside without griping. Looking at his face in the car's weak interior light, before he got out, I realized that he was scared. He opened the hood and we turned off the light so as not to waste the battery. We couldn't see what he was doing, but suddenly we heard him slam the hood down and run to get back into the car, sweat streaming down his neck.

"A snake went over my foot!" he shouted, and his voice broke as if he had phlegm in his throat. Natalia didn't feel like pretending anymore and she laughed at him, pounding the steering wheel with her fists.

"You're a real idiot," she told him, and she dried the tears from her laughter.

"An idiot!" shouted Juan Martín. "What if it had bit me, and it was poisonous, what would we do then, huh? We're in the middle of nowhere!"

"Nothing's going to bite you, take it easy."

"What do you know?"

"More than you."

The three of us were silent. I listened to Juan Martín's breathing and I silently swore that I was never going to have sex with him again, not even if he held a gun to my head. Natalia got out of the car and told us to keep the windows rolled up if we didn't want bugs to get in. "You'll die of heat, but it's one thing or the other." Juan Martín grabbed his head and told me, "Never again, we're never coming here again, you understand me?" Natalia was walking on the empty road and I shined the flashlight on her from inside the car. She was smoking and thinking; I knew her. Juan Martín tried to start the car again, but it sounded more labored and slow than before. "I'm sure your cousin forgot to put water in it," he told me. "No," I replied, "because the car isn't overheated, didn't you see that when you looked at the motor? What *did* you see, huh? You don't know anything, Juan Martín." And I stretched out in the backseat, took off my shirt, and lay there in only my bra.

Once, we had made this same trip with my uncle Carlos and my mom. I don't remember why they needed to go to Asunción. They'd sung songs the whole way there, I remembered that for sure: local songs of legend, love, and loss like "El Puente Pexoa," "El Pájaro Chogui," and "El Cosechero." On the way I had to pee, and I couldn't bring myself to pull down my shorts behind a tree. We pulled into a service station, my uncle asked the attendant for the key, and I went into the little bathroom on the side of the building, the one the truckers used. That little bathroom still haunts my dreams. The smell was brutal. There were fingerprints of shit on the sky-blue tiles; with no toilet paper in sight, many people had used their hands to wipe. How could they do such a thing? The black lid of the toilet was full of bugs. Locusts, mostly, and crickets. They made a terrible noise, a buzzing that sounded like the motor of a refrigerator. I ran out crying, and I pulled down my shorts and peed beside the service station. I didn't say a word about it to my uncle or my mother. I never told them about the stagnant shit in the toilet, the handle dirty with brown fingerprints, the green locusts that almost completely covered the single bulb hanging from the ceiling with no shade over it. After the bathroom I don't remember anything about that trip. My mother talked about how we'd stopped at a beautiful colonial hotel, but how at night you could see rats running around in the yard. I have absolutely no memory of that hotel, or of the rain and hail that had burst over us afterward and delayed our return. That trip, for me, ended in the locust-filled bathroom.

Juan Martín was saying he could walk down the road to who knows what place he had seen lit up, and I didn't answer. If he was afraid of snakes, how was he ever going to make it there? The creatures were constantly going back and forth across the road. Natalia had finished her cigarette—at least, you could no longer see its tip burning in the darkness like one more firefly—but she didn't get back into the car. She wanted to wait outside in case a car passed, sure. Someone who would take her to a phone so she could call the automobile club, for example. Plus, she couldn't have felt much like being in the car with the two of us, and who could blame her after she'd tolerated a whole day of Juan Martín, not to mention me and my passivity.

The lights of the truck lit up the road and the wheels raised a cloud of dust. It was strange because up there in the north, in spite of the heat, there was almost never dry dust in the air because it rained a lot, if not every day. It was always humid and the dirt stuck fast to the ground. But that was how it pulled up: as if borne along on a sandstorm. Natalia had set out the beacon, a triangle that shone phosphorescent in the night, but you could tell she didn't have faith in it because she opened the door, grabbed the flashlight from the driver's seat, and started to wave her arms and shout "Hey, hey, help, help!" I didn't see the driver's face: it was a trailer truck and Natalia had to climb up to talk to him when he stopped, without turning off the motor. Two minutes later, she grabbed her purse and cigarettes and said the guy was going to take her to the service station to call for help. He'd also told her we were close to Clorinda, and that he couldn't bring all three of us because there wasn't enough room. The truck disappeared along the dark road as suddenly as it had arrived, and I realized all the things I hadn't asked Natalia: how long would it take, was the service station nearby, why didn't they go to Clorinda if it was close, did the trucker seem trustworthy, what should we do if another truck or even a car came by—should we stop it?

"We forgot to ask her to get water," said Juan Martín, and it was the first sensible thing he'd said since morning.

My heart started to beat faster: What if we got dehydrated? I rolled down the windows without giving a thought to the bugs. What could they be, other than moths, beetles, crickets? Maybe a bat. Juan Martín said, "Your cousin is irresponsible. She brings us all the way out here where no cars ever pass without even making sure this wreck could run."

"How do you know whether she took the car in?" I asked him, furious, and I thought it would be easy to kill him right there; I could get a screwdriver from the trunk and stab it into his neck. I knew he didn't want to kill me, he just wanted to treat me badly and break me so I'd hate my life and wouldn't even have the guts left to change it. He started to turn on the radio and I almost told him to stop, we had to conserve the battery, but then I let him do it. I was enjoying his ignorance; how I was going to relish it when the tow truck came and he had to explain that he'd used up the battery looking for who knows what on the radio. What could be on the radio around there at night? *Chamamé* and more *chamamé*, and some lonely people who called in and cried and remembered their children who had died in the Malvinas.

The rescue mechanics arrived an hour later. As I'd imagined, they chastised Juan Martín for having the radio on. He sputtered excuses. The mechanics got to work and Juan Martín acted like he was supervising them. I got out and took Natalia's hand.

"You can't even imagine what a hottie the trucker is. One of those Swedes from Oberá. I mean this guy is smoking. He's going to spend the night in Clorinda, and I think I'll stay with him. If the car gets going, that idiot husband of yours can take you to Corrientes," she said to me in a low voice.

But the car didn't start and they had to tow the three of us to Clorinda. The car stayed in the city's automobile club branch, but the mechanics very kindly took us to the hotel Natalia directed them to, pompously called The Ambassador. It was white and had colonial arches, but I knew, just from looking at it from outside, that it was going to smell of damp and maybe wouldn't have hot water. It had a restaurant, though, or more like a grill, with white plastic tables where a family and several solitary men were sitting. "We're going to shower," I told Juan Martín, "and then let's get something to eat."

As they were handing us the hotel keys, a man who could only be the trucker came into the reception area. Natalia went skipping over to him like a teenager. The guy was two heads taller than her, and had muscled arms and blond hair cut very short. "Hello," he said to us, and he smiled. He seemed charming but he could be anything, a degenerate, a wife beater, a rapist—since he was extremely good looking, any girl would rather see him as a golden prince of the highway. I greeted him; Juan Martín took the key and looked at me so I would follow him. I did. Natalia called after me that we'd meet up in an hour to eat and I thought: how tragic, she gets an hour with that sweet-smiling Viking, while I spend an hour tolerating my husband.

Juan Martín yelled at me: "Not once, not even once did you take my side, do you realize? Not about anything. All day long." He shouted that Natalia was a whore, that she went off with the first guy who crossed her path. He shouted that I was a whore too because I'd been making eyes at the goddamn blond barbarian. I told him that blond barbarian had rescued us on the highway, and that at the very least he could have thanked him. "You're rude," I yelled. "You're coarse."

"*I'm* coarse? You fucking little brat," he shouted, and he went into the bathroom and slammed the door. From there he shouted more and cursed because there was no hot water and because the towels reeked of mildew, and finally he came out and threw himself on the bed. "You have nothing to say."

"What do you want me to say?" I answered.

"You may want to leave me now," he said, "but you'll see when we get back to Buenos Aires, things will be better."

"What if they aren't?" I asked him.

"You're not going to leave me that easy," he said, and he lit a cigarette. I took a cold shower and thought that maybe, when I came out, he would have fallen asleep and the cigarette would have lit the sheets on fire and he would die there, in the Clorinda hotel. But when I came out, cold and wet, my blond hair dripping and pathetic, he was waiting for me dressed and perfumed to go to dinner.

"I'm sorry," he told me. "Sometimes I'm impossible."

"Let's go eat," I said, and I put on a loose dress and barely dragged a comb through my hair. I wanted the blond trucker to see me like that, freshly bathed and a bit disheveled. When Juan Martín tried to kiss me, I turned my cheek. But he didn't say anything—he resigned himself.

In the grill there were only two men, my cousin, and the blond trucker left. A dark-haired girl asked us what we wanted and said there was only short ribs, chorizo (she could make sandwiches), and mixed salad. We said yes to everything and ordered a cold soda. I was more thirsty than hungry, even though at the entrance to Clorinda I'd bought a grapefruit Fanta that was nice and cold. It was my favorite soda; for some reason you couldn't get it anymore in Buenos Aires, but it still existed in the interior—maybe they were old bottles, or maybe they still produced it there. Things took longer to disappear up there in the north.

The men were telling ghost stories. Natalia was sitting very close to the blond guy, and they were sharing a cigarette. He had opened his white shirt a little; he was tanned, he was marvelous.

"Something really strange happened to me not long ago," said the splendid blond.

"Tell us, buddy, no one's sleeping here!" shouted another one of the truckers, who was drinking beer. Was he going to get back on the road like that, half drunk? There were always accidents out on these roads, and this was probably why. My uncle Carlos, for example, never got behind the wheel if he was wasted, but he was an exception among his friends and even in our family.

"Should I tell it?" asked the blond, and he looked at my cousin. Natalia smiled at him and nodded.

"Okay," he agreed, and he told us that he came from Oberá province, he lived in Misiones, and that around twenty kilometers away there was a town called Campo Viera. A creek ran through it, the Yazá. "One afternoon, the middle of the day, right? Don't get the idea I imagined this because it was night. I wasn't drunk, either. So, one afternoon I went out there in the small truck, just to run an errand was all, and as I was driving over the Yazá bridge I saw this woman run across the road. I didn't have time to swerve, I would've killed myself, and I felt the bump from her body, man. I jumped out of the truck and ran to her, cold sweat all down my back, but I didn't see anyone. No blood, no dented fender, nothing. I went to the cops and they took my statement, but they were in a shitty mood about it. I had to run the errand another day, and when I was in Campo Viera I told the story just like I'm telling you. They told me that the military had built that bridge, and they'd put dead people in the cement, people they'd murdered, to hide their bodies."

I heard Juan Martín sigh. He didn't like this kind of story.

"You shouldn't fuck around when it comes to things like that," he told the blond guy.

"Excuse me, sir, but I'm not fucking around. The military is perfectly capable of hiding their corpses that way."

Our food came and Juan Martín started to eat. They brought us wooden plates. I've always preferred those to ceramic ones for eating barbecue. The flavor is richer and the oil on the salad is absorbed better and doesn't reach the meat. It was delicious.

The blond guy said that in Campo Viera they'd told him a lot of other things about the bridge and the stream. "That whole area is strange," he said. "You see car headlights but the cars never come, like they've disappeared down some road. But there are no drivable roads, it's all jungle."

"Speaking of cars that disappear, here's a funny one," said one of the other truck drivers, smiling, maybe to clear away the heavy atmosphere and my husband's antipathy. I felt ashamed again and I smiled at the blond truck driver, who had a delicious dimple in his chin, and he smiled back at me. Hopefully he'd become Natalia's boyfriend, and then she'd get bored with him like she did with all of them and then he would realize that always, from the very first moment when we'd looked into each other's eyes in the hotel lobby, he'd been in love with me.

"And it happened right here! Well, at the grill off the highway, ten blocks from here. So this guy comes with his mobile home, a real pretty little house. He was with his family, two kids, they told me, and his wife and mother-in-law. So they went to eat some barbecue and they left the mother-in-law in the mobile home. She didn't feel good or something like that."

"Then what?" asked the third truck driver, who looked sleepy.

"Someone swiped the mobile home with the old lady in it!"

Everyone laughed hard, even the waitress, who was tending the fire as it died down. The guy had been desperate; he'd run to the police and he spent about a week in Clorinda, with his wife having a nervous breakdown. There was a massive search all over Formosa and they found the mobile home, but it was empty. Everything had been stolen, including the mother-in-law.

"How long ago was this?" Natalia wanted to know.

"Hmm . . . must be a year ago now. Time sure flies. A year. It was a crazy case. I'm sure the thieves got into the mobile home and they didn't realize the old lady was inside and maybe she died on them from the fright, and then they tossed her. Around here you can just toss anyone, there's no way in hell they'll find you."

"The man still calls all the time," the girl from the restaurant broke in. "But the woman never turned up."

"The thieves didn't either," added the trucker. "Poor gal, what a way to go."

They went on for a while talking about the mother-in-law's disappearance, and Juan Martín, annoyed, excused himself and went up to the room. *I'll wait for you,* said his look, and I nodded. But I stayed there until very late; my hair dried and the girl gave us the key to the fridge so we could go on taking out beers. Natalia even told the story about the burning house she'd seen from her boyfriend's plane, although she said he was her cousin. Then she yawned and announced she was going up to sleep. The blond trucker followed her. I went after them to the reception desk and asked for another room. I told the girl that my husband was very tired and that if I went in at that hour, I'd wake him up. Then the next day, if the mechanic brought the car, he would have to drive to Buenos Aires badly rested, because he had a hard time going back to sleep when someone woke him up. "Sure," said the woman at reception—it was all women at that hotel, apparently—"we hardly have any guests, it's the low season."

"Low season is right," I told her, and when I laid my head down on the pillow, I fell asleep immediately and had nightmares about an old woman who was running, naked and engulfed in flames, through a house that was collapsing. I saw her from outside, but I couldn't go in and help her because a beam was going to fall and hit my head, or the fire would get to me or the smoke would suffocate me. But I didn't run for help, either; I just watched her burn.

THE AUTO CLUB brought our car in the morning. They explained the problem, but in very general terms, taking it as given that neither Natalia nor I would understand anything. The only thing we wanted to know was if it would make it to Corrientes, and he told us sure, it was only three hours away. We'd still need to take it in to get a more permanent fix, but any mechanic would realize the problem right away and if not, we should call them. We thanked them and went to have breakfast. There was only toast and coffee—not even a croissant—but it was fine. The blond trucker had left two hours earlier. He'd promised to call Natalia and she thought he would come through. "He fucks like a god," she told me. "And he's the sweetest guy."

I envied her. I choked down the half-cold coffee with my tears and went to find Juan Martín. But when I went into the room, he wasn't there. The bed wasn't even unmade, as if he hadn't slept there. I couldn't be sure he had gone back to the room; I hadn't even seen him go into the hotel. I went back to the breakfast room and asked Natalia. "I definitely saw him go inside," she said. The girl at reception assured us he had taken the key with him. At least, she definitely didn't have it hanging on the key rack on the wall.

"Maybe he went for a walk," she murmured.

But, of course, she hadn't seen him come down. I got nervous and my hands started shaking. I told Natalia we had to call the police, but she put her hair back into a ponytail like she'd done in the market and told me no. "Don't be silly. If he left, he left," she said.

She stood up and went to her room to get her purse and the bags with yesterday's purchases.

"You look spooked, babe."

It was true. I was disconcerted. I went back to the room where Juan Martín should have slept, and I didn't see his bag or his toothbrush that he always placed meticulously in the bathroom when we traveled. The shower was dry. The still-damp towels were the ones I had used the night before.

"It's going to rain," said the front-desk girl as she waved good-bye. "That's what the radio says, but it sure doesn't look like it, the sky's all clear."

"I hope it does. This sticky heat is something awful," answered Natalia.

"What about your friend's husband?" she asked as if I weren't right there.

"Oh, there was a misunderstanding."

I settled into the passenger seat. Before leaving Clorinda we stopped at the service station. Natalia needed cigarettes and I needed another grapefruit Fanta. One of the truckers from the night before, the one who'd been sleepy and barely listened to the others' stories, was gassing up. He waved to us, asked how we were, and looked into the backseat. He was probably looking for Juan Martín, but he didn't ask about him. We smiled and waved good-bye, and headed out to the highway. On the horizon along the river, you could already see the black clouds of the gathering storm.

## End of Term

We'd never really paid her much attention. She was one of those girls who don't talk much, who don't stand out for being too smart or too dumb and who have those forgettable faces. Faces you see every day in the same place, but that you might not even recognize if you ever saw them out of context, much less be able to put a name to them. The only striking thing about her was how badly she dressed. Ugly clothes, but something else, too; it looked like she deliberately chose clothes that would hide her body. Two or three sizes too big, shirts buttoned up to the very top button, jeans so loose you couldn't guess at the figure beneath them. Only her clothes caught our attention, and only long enough for us to comment on her bad taste or declare that she dressed like an old lady. Her name was Marcela. She could have been a Mónica, a Laura, a María Jose, or a Patricia, any one of those interchangeable names that the girls no one notices tend to have. She was a bad student, but her teachers rarely failed her. She missed school a lot, but no one mentioned her absence. We didn't know if she had money, what her parents did for a living, what neighborhood she lived in.

We didn't care about her.

Until one day in history class, one of the girls let out a little shriek of disgust. Was it Guada? It sounded like Guada's voice, and she sat near Marcela. While the teacher was explaining the Battle of Caseros, Marcela was pulling the fingernails off her left hand. With her teeth. As if they were press-on nails. Her fingers were bleeding, but she didn't seem to feel any pain. Some girls threw up. The history teacher called in the principal, who took Marcela away; she was absent for a week and no one explained anything to us. When she came back, she wasn't the girl we ignored anymore—she was famous. Some girls were afraid of her, others wanted to be her friend. What she had done was the strangest thing we'd ever seen. Some girls' parents wanted to call a meeting to address the case, because they weren't sure it was a good idea for us to be around an "unbalanced" girl. But they found a compromise. There wasn't much time left in the year, and then we'd be out of high school. Marcela's parents assured everyone she would be OK, that she was taking medication, going to therapy, that she was under control. The other parents believed them. Mine barely paid any attention; they only cared about my grades, and I was still the best student in the class, just like every other year.

Marcela was fine for a while. She came back to school with her fingers bandaged, first with white gauze and later with Band-Aids. She didn't seem to remember the episode of the torn-off fingernails. She didn't make friends with the girls who tried to get close to her. In the bathroom, the ones who'd wanted to be Marcela's friends told us it was impossible because she didn't talk. She listened to them but never answered, and she stared at them so intently that it scared them.

It was also in the bathroom that everything really got

started. Marcela was looking at herself in the mirror, in the only part of it where you could really see anything, since the rest was all peeling, dirty, or covered in marker or lipstick graffiti: declarations of love or obscenities scrawled after some fight between two furious girls. I was with my friend Agustina; we were trying to resolve an argument we'd had earlier. It had seemed like an important discussion, until Marcela took a razor from who knows where (her pocket, I guess). With exacting speed, she sliced a neat cut into her cheek. It took a second for the blood to come, but when it did it practically gushed out, drenching her neck and her shirt that was buttoned all the way up, like a nun's or a dapper man's.

Neither of us moved. Marcela went on looking at herself in the mirror, studying the wound, showing no sign of pain. That was what most impressed me: it clearly didn't hurt her—she hadn't even flinched or closed her eyes. We reacted only when a girl who'd been peeing in a stall opened the door and cried out, "What happened?!" and tried to use her scarf to stop the blood. Agustina looked like she was about to start crying. My knees were trembling. Marcela's smile, as she looked at herself and pressed the scarf to her face, was beautiful. Her face was beautiful. I offered to go with her to her house or to a doctor so they could stitch her up or disinfect the wound. She finally seemed to react then, shaking her head and saying she'd take a taxi. We asked her if she had money. She said yes and smiled again. A smile that could make anyone fall in love. She was absent again for a week. The entire school knew about the incident; no one talked about anything else. When she came back, we all tried not to look at the bandage covering half her face, but no one could help it.

Now I tried to sit near her in class. The only thing I wanted was for her to talk to me, to explain it all to me. I wanted to visit her house. I wanted to know everything. Someone told me they were talking about putting her away. I imagined the hospital with a gray marble fountain in the yard, and violet and brown plants, begonias, honeysuckle, jasmine—I didn't picture a mental hospital that was sordid and dirty and sad, I imagined a beautiful clinic full of empty-eyed women staring off into the distance.

Sitting beside her, I saw what was happening just like everyone else did, only from close up. We all saw it, and we were scared and astonished. It started with her trembling, which wasn't trembling so much as startled jumping. She shook her hands in the air as if to scare something invisible away, as if she were trying to keep something from hitting her. Then she started to cover her eyes and shake her head no. The teachers saw it, but they tried to ignore it. We did too. It was fascinating. She was shamelessly breaking down right in front of us, and it was *us*, the other girls, who were embarrassed.

Not long after that she started pulling out her hair from the front of her head. Whole locks of it piled up on her seat, little mounds of straight blond hair. After a week you could see her scalp, pink and shining.

I was sitting next to her the day she got up and ran out of the classroom. Everyone watched her go; I followed. After a while I noticed that my friend Agustina had come out behind me, and so had the girl who had helped in the bathroom that time, Tere. We felt responsible. Or we wanted to see what she would do, how it all was going to end.

We found her in the bathroom again. It was empty. She was crying and screaming like a child having a tantrum. The bandage had fallen off her face and we could see the stitches in her wound. She was pointing toward one of the toilet stalls and shouting, "Go away, leave me alone, go away." There was something in the air, like too much light, and it smelled more than usual of blood, piss, and disinfectant. I spoke to her:

"What's wrong, Marcela?"

"Don't you see him?"

"Who?"

"Him. Him! There in the stall. Don't you see him?"

She looked at me, anxious and scared but not confused; she saw something. But there was nothing on the toilet, just the beat-up lid and the handle, which was too still, abnormally still.

"No, I don't see anything, there's nothing there," I told her.

Disconcerted for a moment, she grabbed my arm. She'd never touched me before. I looked at her hand; her nails still hadn't grown in, or maybe she pulled them off as they grew. You could only see the bloodied cuticles.

"No? No?" And, looking toward the stall again: "But he's there. He's there. Talk to her, say something to her."

I was afraid the handle would start to move, but it stayed still. Marcela seemed to be listening, looking attentively toward the toilet. I noticed that she had almost no eyelashes left, either. She'd pulled them out. I figured that soon she'd start in on her eyebrows.

"You don't hear him?"

"No."

"But he's talking to you!"

"What's he saying? Tell me."

At this point, Agustina butted into the conversation, telling me to leave Marcela alone, asking me if I was crazy, didn't I see no one was there? "Don't play along with her, I'm scared, let's call someone." She was interrupted by Marcela, who howled,

"SHUT UP, YOU FUCKING BITCH." Tere, who was pretty posh, murmured in English that it was all *just too much*, and she went to find help. I tried to get the situation under control.

"Just ignore those morons, Marcela. What did he say?"

"That he's not going anywhere. That he's real. That he's going to keep making me do things and I can't say no."

"What does he look like?"

"He's a man, but he's wearing a communion dress. His arms are behind him. He's always laughing. He looks Chinese but he's tiny. His hair is slicked back. And he makes me."

"He makes you what?"

When Tere came back with a teacher she'd persuaded to come into the bathroom (later she told us that there'd been around ten girls gathered at the door, listening to everything and shushing each other), Marcela was about to show us what the man with slicked-back hair made her do. But the teacher's sudden appearance confused her. She sat down on the floor, her lashless eyes unblinking as she said, "no."

Marcela never came back to school.

I decided to visit her. It wasn't hard to find her address. Though her house was in a neighborhood I'd never been to, it was easy to reach. I rang the bell with a trembling hand. On the bus there I'd rehearsed an explanation for my visit to give her parents, but now it seemed stupid, ridiculous, forced.

I was struck dumb when Marcela opened the door, not just by the surprise that she was the one to answer—I'd imagined her drugged up and in bed—but also because she looked very different, with a wool cap covering her head that was surely bald by now, jeans, and a normal-sized sweater. Except for her eyelashes, which hadn't grown in yet, she looked like a healthy, normal girl.

She didn't invite me in. She came outside, closed the door behind her, and the two of us stayed in the street. It was cold; she wrapped her arms around herself, and my ears stung.

"You shouldn't have come," she said.

"I want to know."

"What do you want to know? I'm not going back to school; it's over, forget the whole thing."

"I want to know what he makes you do."

Marcela looked at me and sniffed at the air around her. Then she looked off toward the window. The curtains had moved a little. She went back into her house and, before she slammed the door, she said:

"You'll find out. He's going to tell you himself one of these days. He's going to make you do it too, I think. Soon."

On the way back, sitting on the bus, I felt the throb of the wound I had cut into my thigh with a box cutter the night before, under the sheets. It didn't hurt. I massaged my leg gently, but hard enough that the blood as it spilled drew a fine, damp line on my light blue jeans.

## No Flesh over Our Bones

I saw it as I was about to cross the street. It was lying in a pile of garbage, abandoned among the roots of a tree. Dentistry students, I thought, those soulless and stupid people, ignoramuses who think only about money and are steeped in bad taste and sadism. I picked it up with both hands in case it fell apart. The skull was missing its jaw and every one of its teeth, a mutilation that confirmed it was indeed the work of the proto-dentists. I looked around the tree and went through all the garbage. I couldn't find the teeth. What a shame, I thought, and I walked to my apartment just two hundred meters away, holding the skull in my hands like I was processing toward a pagan forest ceremony.

I put it on the living room table. It was small. The skull of a child? I'm ignorant of all things anatomical and osseous. For example, I don't understand why skulls don't have noses. When I touch my face, I feel my nose stuck to my skull. Maybe the nose is cartilage? I don't think so, although it's true they say it doesn't hurt when it breaks and that it breaks easily, like a weak bone. I examined the skull more closely and found it had a name written on it. And a number. *Tati, 1975.* So many possibilities. Could be its name, Tati, born in 1975. Or its owner could be a Tati, who came into existence in 1975. Or maybe the number wasn't a date but had to do with some kind of classification. Out of respect I decided to baptize it with the generic name Calavera, which means "skull" in Spanish. By the time my boyfriend came home from work that night, she was already just Vera.

He, my boyfriend, didn't see her until he took off his jacket and sat down on the sofa. He is a very unobservant man.

When he saw her, he gave a startled jump but didn't get up. He is also lazy, and he's getting fat. I don't like fat men.

"What is that? Is it real?"

"Of course it's real," I told him. "I found it in the street. It's a skull."

He yelled at me then. "Why would you bring it here?" he shouted at me in a somewhat exaggerated manner. "Where did you get it?" It struck me that he was making a scene, and I ordered him to lower his voice. I tried to explain to him calmly that I had found her discarded in the street, abandoned under a tree, and that it would have been totally indecent on my part to act with indifference and just leave her there.

"You're crazy."

"Maybe so," I told him, and I brought Vera into my room.

He waited a while then, in case I came out to make him dinner. He doesn't need to eat anything else; he's getting fat. His thighs already rub against each other and if he wore a woman's skirt he would always be chafed between his legs. After an hour I heard him curse me and call to order a pizza. How lazy. He'd rather get delivery than walk downtown and eat in a restaurant. It costs almost the same.

"Vera, I don't know what I'm doing with him."

If she could talk, I know she would tell me to leave him. It's common sense. Before I go to sleep I spray my favorite perfume over the bed, and I put a little on Vera, under her eyes and along her sides.

Tomorrow I'll buy her a little wig. To keep my boyfriend out of the room, I turn the key in the lock.

My boyfriend says he's afraid and other nonsense like that. He sleeps in the living room, but it's not a sacrifice because the futon I bought with my money—he doesn't make much—is of excellent quality. "What are you afraid of?" I ask him. He sputters inanities about how I spend all my time locked in with Vera, how he hears me talking to her.

I ask him to move out, to pack his things and leave the apartment, to leave me. His expression is one of profound pain; I don't believe it and I almost push him into the bedroom so he can pack his suitcases. He screams again, but this time it's a scream of fear. He's seen my pretty Vera, who is wearing her pricey blond wig made of natural hair, fine and yellow, surely cut in some ex-Soviet village in Ukraine or the steppes (are Siberian women blond?), the braids of some girl who still hasn't found anyone to take her away from her miserable village. I find it very strange that poor blondes exist, which is why I bought her that one. I also bought her some necklaces with colored beads, very festive. And she's surrounded by aromatic candles, the kind that women who aren't like me put in the bathroom or the bedroom while they wait for some man among flames and rose petals.

He threatened to call my mother. I told him he could do what he wanted. He looked fatter than ever, with his cheeks hanging down like a Neapolitan mastiff's, and that night, after he left carrying his suitcase and with a bag slung over his shoulder, I decided to stop eating much, to eat very little. I thought about beautiful bodies like Vera's, if she were whole: white bones that shine under the light in forgotten graves, thin bones that sound like little party bells when they hit against each other, frolicking in the fields, doing dances of death. He has nothing to do with the ethereal beauty of those naked bones: his are covered with layers of fat and boredom. Vera and I will be beautiful and light, nocturnal and earthy; beautiful, the crusts of earth enfolding us. Hollow, dancing skeletons. Vera and I—no flesh over our bones.

A week after giving up food, my body changes. If I raise my arms my ribs show through, although not much. I dream: someday, when I sit on this wooden floor, instead of buttocks I'll have bones, and the bones will poke through the flesh and leave bloodstains on the floor, they'll slice through the skin from inside.

I BOUGHT VERA SOME FAIRY LIGHTS, the kind people use to decorate Christmas trees. I couldn't keep seeing her there without eyes, or rather, with dead eyes, so I decided that in her empty sockets some little lamps would shine. Since they're colored I can alternate them, and one day Vera can have red eyes, another day green, and another day blue. While I was lying on the bed and contemplating the effect of Vera with eyes, I heard some keys opening my apartment door. My mother, the only person who had a key, because I'd made my obese ex give his back. I got up to let her in. I made tea and sat down to drink it with her. "You're thinner," she said to me. "It's the stress of the separation," I replied. We fell silent. Finally she spoke:

"Patricio told me you're into something strange."

"Into what? Please, Mom, he's making things up because I kicked him out."

"He says you're obsessed with a skull."

I laughed.

"He's crazy. With some of my girlfriends we're making costumes and scary decorations for Halloween; it's just for fun. I didn't have time to buy a costume, so I put together a voodoo tableau and I'm going to buy some other things: black candles, a crystal ball, to set the scene, you know? Because we're having the party here at my house."

I don't know how much she understood, but she thought it was a reasonable bit of nonsense. She wanted to meet Vera, and I showed her. She thought it was morbid that I had her in the bedroom, but she totally believed the story about decorating for the party, even though I've never thrown a party in my life and I detest birthdays. She also believed my lies about Patricio's vindictiveness.

She was reassured when she left, and I know she won't be back for a while. That's quite all right with me; I want to be alone. Vera's incompleteness has put me on edge. She can't stay like that, with no teeth, no arms, no spine. I'm never going to find the bones that went with her head when she was alive, that's obvious. I'll have to study anatomy to find out the names and shapes of the bones she's missing, which are all of them. And where should I look for them? I can't desecrate graves, I wouldn't know where to start. My father used to talk about common graves in the cemeteries of Buenos Aires that were open to the sky like pools full of bones, but I don't think those exist anymore, not these days. And if they existed, wouldn't they have guards? He told me that medical students used to go there to find skeletons to use for studying. Where do they get them now, the bones for anatomy classes? Or do they use plastic replicas? It seems to me it would be difficult to walk through the streets carrying a human bone. If I find one, I'll carry it in the big backpack that Patricio left, the one we took camping when he was still thin. We all walk over bones in this city, it's just a question of making holes deep enough to reach the buried dead. I have to dig, with a shovel, with my hands, like a dog. Dogs always find bones; they always know where they're hidden, where they've been abandoned, forgotten.

## The Neighbor's Courtyard

Paula looked at her hands, reddened and scored from carrying several big crates of books, while Miguel paid and said good-bye to the moving men. She was hungry, she was tired, but she loved the house. They'd been very lucky. The rent wasn't high and they had three bedrooms: one would be the study; another, their bedroom; the third would probably be for visitors. In the yard, the previous tenant had left behind simple and very pretty plants, a large cactus and a tall, healthy climbing plant of a strange, very dark green. And the best part was that the house had a roof terrace, with a grill and space to set up a covered picnic area if the owner didn't mind—and Paula thought she would let them make any reasonable modification they wanted. On one hand, she'd seemed like a very friendly and easygoing woman ("In the contract it says that you can't have pets, but just ignore that, I love animals"), and on the other, Paula thought she seemed anxious to get the place rented. She'd accepted them with only one co-signer—Miguel's mother; usually, landlords asked for two—and with only one salary, also Miguel's, because

Paula was temporarily out of work. Maybe the landlady needed the money, or she wanted the house to be occupied before it started to deteriorate from lack of upkeep.

Her attitude had made Miguel a little suspicious, and before signing the contract he had asked if they could visit the house one more time. He hadn't found anything troubling: the bathroom worked perfectly, although they'd have to change the shower curtain because it was mildewed. The house had a lot of light, it wasn't noisy even though it looked out onto the street, and the neighborhood with its lines of low houses seemed quite calm, but busy, with a lot of people in the shops along the street and even a modest bar on the corner. He had to admit he'd been paranoid. Paula, on the other hand, had trusted from the start in the house and its owner. She already knew where the desk and the books would go, and she was looking forward to studying outside in the courtyard, buying a comfortable chair so she could sit out there with her papers and a cup of coffee. Her plan was to finish her degree, take the three exams that she still needed to graduate, all within a year, and then go back to work. Finally she was setting a timeline, planning the months to come, and the house seemed ideal for her mission.

They unpacked boxes and stacked books until the mess became unbearable and they ordered a pizza. They ate in the courtyard with the radio on. Miguel hated the first few days in a new house, when there was still no TV or Internet, and he was in an anticipatory bad mood thinking of the calls he would have to make before everything was in order. But he was too tired to worry. After smoking a cigarette, he went inside to lie down on the mattress, still without sheets, where he fell asleep. Paula fought sleep a while longer and brought the radio up to the roof to listen to a little music under the stars. She could see the buildings along the avenue very close by; in a few years, she thought, houses like hers—she already felt it was hers—were going to be bought and demolished to put up tall buildings. The neighborhood wasn't in fashion yet, but it was only a matter of time. It wasn't too far from downtown, it had a subway station nearby and a reputation for being quiet. She'd have to enjoy it as long as the rest of the city remained indifferent.

The terrace was edged by low walls, but it also had a fairly high mesh fence. Likely the owner had once had a dog there—that was why she'd mentioned her love for animals—and the mesh was to keep it from escaping. In one corner, though, the mesh had fallen. From there it was possible to look over and just see a sliver of the neighbor's courtyard, four or five red tiles. She went downstairs to find a light blanket to cover herself in bed: the night had grown cool.

THE POUNDING THAT WOKE HER UP was so loud she doubted it was real; it had to be a nightmare. It was making the house shake. The banging on the front door sounded like punches thrown by enormous hands, the hands of a beast, a giant's fists. Paula sat up in bed and felt her face burning and the sweat soaking the back of her neck. In the darkness the pounding sounded like something was about to get in, about to break down the door. She turned on the light. Miguel was sleeping! It was incredible; maybe he was sick, or he'd fainted. She shook him brutally awake, but by then the pounding had stopped.

"What's wrong?"

"You didn't hear it?"

"What's wrong, Pau? Why are you crying, what's going on?"

"I can't believe it didn't wake you up. Didn't you hear the pounding on the door? They almost kicked it in!"

"The front door? I'll go check."

"No!"

Paula had shouted. A snarling shout, animal in its terror. Miguel turned around while he was pulling on his pants and told her:

"Let's not start."

Then Paula clenched her teeth so hard she bit her tongue and started to cry harder. He was giving her that look again, and she knew how this was going to go. First he'd get impatient and then overly understanding, soothing; then, in a little while, Miguel would do what she hated most: he would treat her like she was crazy. *Let him die, then,* she thought. *If there's an armed gang trying to get in, if he's such a dumbass he's going to open the door because he doesn't believe me, let him die. I'll enjoy the house on my own, I'm sick of him.* But Paula got up, ran behind Miguel, and asked him to please not open the door. He saw something in her eyes; he believed her.

"Let's take a look from the terrace. You have to be able to see the street from there."

"The terrace has wire mesh around it."

"I saw, but it's loose, it'll come off easy."

Miguel effortlessly pulled off the wire, which was practically unattached. He leaned boldly out over the roof's edge. There was no one on the sidewalk. The light from the street illuminated the front door of the house and there was no room for doubt. The whole block was well lit. Across the street were two parked cars, but through the windows you could see they were empty. Unless someone was lying down in the backseat to hide, but . . . who would want to stalk them like that?

"Let's go to bed," said Miguel.

Paula followed him, still crying, still furious, but also relieved. She was even happy at having had a too-vivid dream, if that was what it had been. Miguel went back to bed without saying a word. He didn't want to talk, didn't want to argue, and she was grateful.

In the morning the pounding seemed very distant, and Paula resigned herself and accepted that it must have happened in a nightmare. It helped that Miguel had already left for work by the time she got up, so she didn't have to face him or talk about what she had heard. She didn't have to endure his sad expression. It was so unfair. Just because she'd been depressed, like so many people were, and because she took medication—in very low doses—Miguel thought she was sick. She'd been surprised to find out that her husband was so prejudiced, but over the past year it had become clear. At the start of her depression, he'd insisted on getting her out of bed; he told her to go running, or to the gym, or to open the windows, visit her girlfriends. When Paula decided to consult a psychiatrist, Miguel flew into a rage and told her not to even think of going to one of those charlatans. Why did she have to talk to someone else, he asked. Didn't she trust him? He'd even said they probably needed to have a baby. He started talking about her biological clock and a bunch of other weird ideas that at the time hadn't mattered to her, but that when she started to recover had bothered her to the point where she started wondering if she even wanted to stay with Miguel. He had never shown any other kind of prejudice; it was directed exclusively toward psychiatrists, mental problems, madness. They'd talked about it not long ago: Miguel had admitted to her that in his opinion, except for serious illnesses, all emotional problems could be solved by force of will.

"That's some real bullshit," she'd told him. "You really think an obsessive-compulsive person can just stop, I don't know, washing his hands over and over?"

It turned out that Miguel did think so. That an alcoholic could just stop drinking and an anorexic could start eating again if they really wanted to. He was making a huge effort—and he told her so while staring at the floor—to accept her going to a psychiatrist and taking pills, because he thought it was useless and the problem would pass on its own, that it was normal to be sad after the problems she'd had at work.

"But I'm not just sad, Miguel," she'd answered, cold and ashamed. Ashamed of his ignorance, and little disposed to tolerate it.

"I know, I know," he said.

Paula knew that her mother-in-law, who was wonderful and who loved her, had talked to Miguel. More accurately, she'd given him a piece of her mind.

"I don't know, Paula dear, how my son turned out to be such an idiot," she'd said over coffee. "In my house no one thinks like that. If none of us goes to therapy, it's only because, thank God, we don't need it. Although maybe that numbskull son of mine does. I'm truly sorry, dear."

Now she was waiting for her mother-in-law, Monica, who was supposed to come over and drop off Elly, the cat. They'd decided to bring her the day after the move so she wouldn't bother them or get too nervous. Cat and mother-in-law arrived as Paula was finishing arranging pots, plates, and pans in the kitchen. She made coffee for Monica while the cat inspected the new house, sniffing everything, frightened, her tail between her legs.

"It's a beautiful house," said Monica. "So big! And there's so much light, you two really got lucky! It's impossible to rent in Buenos Aires."

She wanted to see the courtyard. She said she'd bring some plants over next time, and she just loved the terrace; she promised meat for a barbecue as soon as they were settled. She left after kissing Paula and the cat, and she left a small bouquet of freesia as a gift. Paula loved her mother-in-law for things like that: for how she didn't stay too long when she visited, how she never criticized except when asked for her opinion, how she knew how to help without overacting.

Since she had first seen the terrace she'd been worried about Elly, because even though the cat was fixed and surely wouldn't wander far, she would probably decide to investigate the rooftops for the first time in her life—she had only ever lived in apartments before. There was nothing Paula could do; it was an unsolvable problem. Not even the mesh would stop a cat—it would only help her climb. It was hot, and Paula went up to the terrace. She didn't feel like studying. Sitting on the wall, she saw an enormous cat, gray with short hair, walk across the neighbor's courtyard. Elly's boyfriend, she thought, and she was happy to have a neighbor with a cat. He could recommend the best veterinarian in the neighborhood and help her look for Elly if she ran away.

That night Miguel still didn't mention the pounding, and she was grateful. They ate a delicious lentil stew from the delicatessen and went to bed early. Miguel was tired and he went right to sleep. Paula had more trouble. She listened to Elly, who still hadn't calmed down and was roaming around the house, attacking boxes with her claws, climbing up crates or onto the stove. And she was waiting for the pounding on the door. She'd left the courtyard light on to shine into the bedroom, so they wouldn't have to sleep in total darkness. The pounding didn't come back.

At some point near dawn, however, she saw that someone very small was sitting at the foot of the bed. At first she thought it must be Elly, but it was too big to be a cat. She couldn't see more than a shadow. It looked like a child, but there was no hair on top of his head; you could clearly see the line where he was balding, and he was very small, thin. More curious than frightened, Paula sat up in bed, and when she did, the supposed child went running out. But he ran too fast to be human. Paula didn't want to think. Surely it had been Elly because it had run like a cat. *It was Elly and I'm half asleep and I don't realize I'm half asleep and I think I'm seeing dwarf-elves, what a moron.* She knew she was going to have trouble going back to sleep, so she took a pill and saw nothing more until she woke up very late the next morning.

THE DAYS PASSED, and Paula and Miguel gradually dealt with the boxes and crates, and neither the pounding nor the dwarf-cat came back. Paula convinced herself that it had been the stress from the move; she'd read once that moving was the third most stressful life event, after the death of a loved one and being fired. In the past two years she'd gone through all three: her father had died, she'd been fired from her job, and she'd moved. And then there was her idiot of a husband, who thought she could get over it all just by trying. How she despised him sometimes. In the calm afternoons in the new house, while she went on organizing and cleaning and studying, sometimes she thought about leaving him. But she had to get her life together before she made any decisions. Finish her sociology degree, first; a pollster friend had already offered her a job at his consulting firm as soon as she graduated. She could start working sooner, of course, but Paula knew she wasn't ready. *Next year, then. I'll go back to work, and if things stay the same with Miguel, it's over.*

She even thought Miguel would be relieved. It had been a year, at least, since they'd had sex. Miguel didn't seem to mind, and she certainly didn't want to. Their life together was bearably calm, but it wasn't friendly. *We need time*, Paula thought; maybe in a year they would even start fucking again, or they'd end up as friends, not actually a couple, and the thing would relax and they could keep living together, the way things happened with so many people who loved each other but weren't in love anymore. For now she had to finish her classes—there were only three, and what she'd read so far hadn't seemed all that complicated.

When she saw it, she was taking a break between one photocopied paper and another, hanging clean clothes from the line on the terrace. Elly was sleeping in the sun; the cat showed no interest in exploring the neighborhood's roofs, and Paula was grateful. She peeked into the neighbor's courtyard, at the maybe five or six flagstones she could see, red and old like those of a colonial house. She was looking for the gray cat she'd never seen again. Could it have died? She never heard it, either. The next-door neighbor was a single man who wore glasses and had a very strange, unpredictable schedule, and who greeted her politely but without warmth. She didn't see the cat, and as she was turning back to the wet clothes, a movement in the courtyard caught her eye. It wasn't the cat; it was a leg. A child's leg, naked, with a chain attached to the ankle. Paula took a deep breath and leaned farther out, almost in danger of falling from the terrace. It was a leg, no doubt about it, and now she could see part of the torso and confirm that it was a child, not an old person. A very thin and completely naked boy; she could see his genitals. His skin was dirty, gray from grime. Paula didn't know whether to shout at him, to go down immediately, or to call the police . . . She'd never seen the chain in the yard before—though it was true she didn't spy on the neighbor's courtyard every day—and she had never heard a child's voice when she was on the terrace.

She clucked as though to call her cat, trying not to alert the boy's jailers, and then the small body down below moved out of her field of vision. But on the five or six flagstones she could still see the chain, motionless now, as if the boy were intent, waiting for her to call again with no way of escaping.

Paula brought her hands to her cheeks. She knew what to do in these cases. She had worked for a long time as a social worker. But after what had happened a year ago—after she'd been fired, after the hearing—she didn't even want to think about taking responsibility again for lost children, damaged children. She ran down the stairs but didn't make it to the bathroom. She threw up in the living room, spattering one of the boxes of books, and she cried sitting down, her straight, loose hair almost brushing the floor, the cat looking at her with her head cocked and her round, green eyes curious.

*It's the boy I saw that night, weeks ago, at the foot of the bed*, she thought. *It's the same one. What was he doing? They let him out sometimes? What do I do?* The first things she did were to clean up the vomit, unload the books, and throw the stinking box into the trash. Then she went back to the terrace to peer into the neighbor's courtyard. The chain was in the same place, but the boy had moved a little and now she could see his foot. There was no doubt it was a human foot, a child's foot. She could call child services, the police; there were many options, but first she wanted Miguel to see him. She wanted him to know, to help her: if Miguel shared the responsibility with her and they managed to do something for the boy, she felt like maybe they could recover something of what they used to have: those years of taking the car wherever they felt like on weekends, to provincial villages in the middle of nowhere, to eat good barbecue and take photos of old houses, or the Sundays of sex, with the mattress on the floor and the marijuana cured with honey that her husband's brother grew.

Paula resolved to be prudent. In nearly a month, it was the first time she'd seen the boy. She wasn't going to bring Miguel running up to the terrace to show him the chain, the foot. The boy could move out of sight, and she didn't want Miguel to doubt her. She would tell him calmly first, and then they'd go up to the terrace together. She was about to call him but she stopped herself. She went up to the terrace several times, and each time she saw the chain or the chain with the foot. She thought of all the stories about children tied to beds, chained up, locked in, that she'd heard in her days as a social worker. She'd never had to work on a case like that; they were rare in the city. People said those children never recovered. That they had terrifying lives and died young; they were too damaged, their scars always visible.

When Miguel came home, a little earlier than usual, she didn't even wait for him to drop his bag on the sofa before she started telling him about the boy. He just kept saying, "What? What?" And she repeated, "The neighbor has a boy chained up in the courtyard, no, it's not that strange, there are a lot of cases like that, it's not crazy, let's go up, let's go up, you'll see, we have to figure out what to do." But when they went together up to the terrace and peered into the neighbor's courtyard, the chain wasn't there anymore. No boy and no leg. Paula whistled, but the only thing that happened was that Elly turned up, meowing happily, thinking she was being called to eat. Miguel did what Paula feared most.

"You're crazy," he said, and went downstairs.

In the kitchen he threw a glass against the wall, and when Paula came in she was met by the glint of glass shards.

"You don't even realize!" he shouted. "You don't realize you're hallucinating! Right, there's going to be a boy chained up in the courtyard. Obviously. You don't get that it's because of your job; you're obsessed."

Paula yelled too, she didn't know what. Insults, justifications. She wanted to stop him when he stormed out and left the door open, but then a luminous calm settled over her. Why was she acting like she really was crazy? Why was she giving Miguel more fuel? He had decided for no reason not to trust her, probably because he wanted to leave her, too. Why was she acting like there was something rational in that argument over her mental health? She had seen a boy in the neighbor's courtyard, and he was in chains. She had never hallucinated before. If Miguel didn't believe her, that was his problem. She went up to the terrace one more time and sat on the wall to wait for the boy to come back into view. Miguel wouldn't come back that night. She didn't care. She had someone to save. She found a flashlight in a box and settled in.

The incident Paula had been fired for was also the result of stress, but sometimes it seemed as though Miguel just couldn't forgive her. As though he'd written her off as a worthless piece of shit, just like her former employers had, like she herself was tempted, at times, to do. That week had gotten off to a terrible start. Paula was the director of a children's shelter on the city's south side. It was a fairly small house, with a damp game room almost empty of games, a TV that provided the only entertainment, a kitchen, and a bedroom with three bunk beds, only six beds in total. That was good; it was too complicated to deal with many young children. Friday night, always a difficult night, they'd called her at home. She was fast asleep, she was tired. They asked her to come in right away because there was a serious problem. She drove there half asleep and found a scene that was unbelievable in its stupidity. One of the kids, around six years old, was very high—he'd arrived the day before when she wasn't working, and no one had searched him carefully; he must have had the drugs on him. He'd shat himself while watching TV. The boy had diarrhea and the game room stank. One of the two supervisors on duty, who was an imbecile, wanted to put the boy back out on the street. According to her the rules said that they didn't have the capacity to deal with addicted children. The fight with the other supervisor, who insisted that throwing the boy out was cruelty, first of all, and abandonment to boot, had almost come to blows. The boy, meanwhile, was drooling in his bed and smearing shit all over the sheets. When Paula arrived she had to yell at the supervisors, explain to the two women how to do their jobs, and then help them clean up—the janitors wouldn't come until the next day. The boy was transferred, and so was the supervisor who'd wanted to throw him out. But, as tends to happen in social services, it would take them a long time to find a replacement. So Paula decided to take over until the new person arrived: twelve-hour shifts that she alternated with the other supervisor and a substitute, an eager young guy named Andrés.

On Wednesday, one of the boys escaped. He managed to climb up to the roof from the kitchen window. It was noon when they realized he'd fled, but they didn't know how long he'd been gone. Paula could clearly remember how she trembled from head to foot thinking about the boy, out in the street again, dodging cars, stealing half-eaten hamburgers. He was a boy from the bus station who surely turned tricks in the bathroom and who, though he was only six, knew all the city's nooks and crannies, down to the criminals' hideouts. A boy who was hard like a war veteran—worse, because he lacked a veteran's pride—and who spoke a deep dialect understood only by the other children and some social workers more experienced than her.

The boy turned up in a hospital that very same night; they called to tell her while she was patrolling Villa 21, where little girls, twelve-year-old addicts, got into trucks to suck the drivers' cocks and make enough money for the next fix. He'd been hit by a car while he was high. But he was fine, hadn't even broken a bone, he was just a little bruised. Paula didn't go see him; Andrés went to visit. That boy was transferred, too. Paula started to feel like they couldn't do the job, like the children were slipping right through her fingers.

The next day a five-year-old girl was brought in. They'd found her in the street with a man and woman who weren't her parents; she was dirty and very tired. She was going to stay at the shelter until her real parents were found or some other legal decision was made. The girl wasn't cagey and sullen like most of the children who passed through the home. She laughed at the

TV until her belly hurt. She talked a lot, and she told them about the games of make-believe she'd played in the street. She talked about a boy-cat she'd met in the botanical gardens, for example, a boy who lived there among the other animals and who had yellow eyes and could see in the dark. She loved cats and wasn't afraid of him: he was her friend. The girl also talked about her mother and said she'd lost her. She didn't know where she lived, only that she got to her house by train. But she couldn't remember which line it was, and when she described the station she mixed up details of the two largest ones in the city. Paula and her colleagues were sure her family would be found soon.

The following Friday, Paula was alone on duty at the shelter all night. Miguel hated it when that happened, but she'd promised it was only until they found a replacement—and she wasn't lying, she didn't like the night shift either. The only children at the shelter were the friendly little girl and an eight-year-old boy who spoke very little but was well behaved. Paula arrived at ten at night to relieve Andrés. The children were already asleep. Andrés, who'd had a hard time of it that week—he also worked at a night service that patrolled the streets in search of children—invited her to share a beer and smoke a joint. Paula accepted. They turned on the radio, too. Later she was told that it was very loud, that even the neighbors had heard it, but at the time it seemed like the volume was normal and she'd be able to hear the doorbell or the phone or the kids if they woke up. They spent a couple of hours drinking and laughing and chatting, that part she conceded. At the time she didn't think she was doing anything wrong: she knew it was incorrect, but she felt like they needed to relax after a difficult week. They were two colleagues having a good time.

She would never forget the look on the supervisor's face

when she came into the kitchen, unplugged the radio with a yank, and yelled: "What the fuck are you doing? What the hell are you motherfuckers doing?" Especially that "you motherfuckers"; it had been so heartfelt, so sincere. Things happened quickly; they had to absorb the information half drunk and high, absolutely guilty. A neighbor had called the supervisor—he had her home number—because he heard a child crying in the shelter. The supervisor thought it was strange because she knew Paula was on duty, as she told the neighbor, but he'd insisted that there was a girl crying and the music was turned up very loud. The part about the music convinced the supervisor, who immediately thought of thieves, of something serious. When she arrived, there was in fact something serious happening, but not what she'd expected. The little girl had simply fallen from her bunk and was crying and wailing on the floor, her ankle broken. The other boy, the silent one, was watching her from his bed but hadn't gone for help. And the music coming from the kitchen was very loud, as if someone was having a party. When she opened the door, she was surprised and angrier than she'd ever been when she saw Paula and Andrés with two empty beer bottles and a smoldering joint in the ashtray, laughing like idiots while a homeless girl who trusted them was screaming in pain from the floor where she'd been lying for at least half an hour.

When the legal proceedings began, the supervisor was merciless. She testified and recommended they both be fired. She was an experienced woman, respected; she got them thrown out almost immediately with no right to appeal. What were they going to say? That they were under stress? And the girl, who had lost her mother in the street, and the mute boy they'd found hidden in a train car—what about them? Were they having a good time? Miguel always told her he understood, that they'd been excessive, they'd been exploiting her; he went with her to the hearings and never judged her aloud. But she knew what he was thinking, because it was the only thing anyone could have thought: she deserved to be fired. She deserved contempt. She had acted irresponsibly, like a cynic, like a brute.

The depression came after she was fired. Unable to get out of bed, unable to sleep or eat or bathe, she cried and cried. A typical depression that had gone too far only once, when she'd mixed pills with alcohol and slept for almost two days straight. But even the psychiatrist recognized that the episode didn't qualify as a suicide attempt. He didn't even suggest admitting her. He enlisted Miguel's help, asked him to keep an eye on when and how much she drank, at least for a while. Miguel did it reluctantly, as if it were a difficult, demanding task. And for him it was, thought Paula. But he was exaggerating; the depression had been intense, but normal. Now she was over it. And he treated her like the crazy woman she had never been, for a different reason: because he'd never forgiven her for abandoning that little girl. He'd never been able to get that image out of his mind: the sobbing in the night, the broken ankle. Or the image of Paula laughing, her mouth reeking of beer. That was why he no longer desired her. Because he'd seen a side of her that was too dark. He didn't want to have sex with her, he didn't want to have children with her, he didn't know what she was capable of. Paula had gone from being a saint—the social worker who specialized in at-risk children, so maternal and selfless—to being a sadistic and cruel public employee who neglected the children while she listened to *cumbia* and got drunk; she'd become the evil directress of a nightmare orphanage.

Fine: what they'd once had was over, then. But she could still do something. She could save the chained-up boy. She was going to save him.

MIGUEL DIDN'T COME BACK THAT NIGHT. The boy didn't show himself, not even his chain. Paula sat on the terrace looking down at the flagstones. From there she heard her husband leave a message on the machine saying that he was at his mother's house, would she please call him, they had to talk, but he needed a few days before he could come back. *Fine, whatever,* thought Paula. It was hot. Elly stayed with her all night long; they slept curled up together on some blankets until the burning morning sun woke them up. Elly wanted water for breakfast, as always, and Paula turned on the tap so she could drink from it; like all cats she loved fresh, running water. Paula almost started crying as she watched her cat, so beautiful, black with her little white feet, sticking out her rough tongue. She loved her more than she loved Miguel, she was sure.

The boy wasn't in the yard, but Paula heard the neighbor's door slam; she ran across the terrace and watched the man, her neighbor, head off toward the avenue. Was he the boy's father? Or had he enslaved the child? . . . She didn't want to think about it too much. She made a demented decision: she would go into the house. She could jump from the terrace into the courtyard. She'd been studying it all night. She'd have to be smart, like a cat: jump onto the dividing wall, and from there onto an old container she could see in the yard—a water heater? something like that, a metal cylinder—and she'd be in. She could call the police from the house once she found the boy.

Getting into the yard was easy, easier than she'd expected. She had a small, normal thought: that meant it would be easy to rob the neighbor's house, and her own. She would think about that later, once she'd done what she had to do.

There were two doors that led from the courtyard into the house: one to the living room, the other to the kitchen. There was no sign of the boy in the courtyard. Not even the chain. There were no bowls with food or water, and no dirt; quite the contrary, it stank of disinfectant or bleach: someone had washed the place down. The boy had to be inside, unless the man had taken him somewhere while she and Miguel were fighting, or in the morning after she'd fallen asleep. Stupid, lazy! How could she fall asleep?

She went into the kitchen, which was dark, and the light wouldn't turn on. She tried other switches, even one in the courtyard; the house didn't have electricity. She was afraid. The kitchen stank. At first, the adrenaline had kept her from feeling the full impact of the atrocious stench. But the counter was clean, and so was the table. Paula opened the refrigerator and didn't find anything strange: mayonnaise, cutlets on a plate, tomatoes. Then she opened the pantry and the smell filled her eyes and made them water, and bitter liquid flooded her throat; her stomach churned desperately and it took a tremendous effort not to throw up. She couldn't see well, but she didn't need to; the pantry was full of rotten meat on which the white maggots of putrescence grew and wriggled. The worst was that she couldn't tell what kind of meat it was: whether it was everyday beef that the man in his madness had left there to rot, or something else. She couldn't make out any human shapes, but really she couldn't make out any shape at all. In the half darkness, it seemed like the meat was living its death right there, growing in the pantry like mold. She ran from the kitchen—she couldn't hold back the nausea any longer—without closing the pantry door. She knew she had to go back, close it, cover her tracks, but she didn't feel capable. Let whatever had to happen, happen.

The rest of the house—foyer, two bedrooms—was all very dark. Still, Paula went into what had to be the man's bedroom. It had no windows. In the shadows she could see that the bed was neatly made and covered with a warm blanket, though it was the middle of summer. The wallpaper had a very subtle design that looked like little signs, an arachnid weave. Paula touched it, and to her surprise she felt the rough paint of the wall. She moved closer and saw that the walls weren't actually papered: they were covered in writing that left almost no white space, an elegant and even script that she had taken for a filigreed motif. She couldn't make out any coherent sentences. There were dates: *March twentieth,* she read; *December tenth.* And some words: *asleep, blue, understanding.* She checked her pockets for her lighter, but she didn't have it. She didn't want to look for one in the kitchen. She thought that once her eyes got more used to the darkness she could read better, but after waiting a few minutes she felt the sweat run down her back and the pain in her head grow stronger and she was afraid she might faint in that horrible house, that house she never should have entered. If she hadn't cared about that beautiful child with her broken ankle—oh, the look on that girl's face when the ambulance took her away, the look of hatred in her eyes; she'd known that Paula was guilty, every bit as evil as the streets—why did she care about that boy she'd glimpsed in the courtyard? A boy who, if he was living with this crazy man, was surely already ruined for good, far beyond any possible recovery or normal life. The compassionate thing to do, if she found him, would be to kill him.

She went into the living room. Also neat and empty, but there she found the chain on a maroon faux-leather sofa. The living room, which led out to the courtyard, had some light. She ventured to speak.

"Hello," she whispered. "Are you there?"

She knew she didn't need to shout in the house: it was small and utterly silent. She waited, but didn't hear anything. She went over to a glass-doored library, where she could make out piles of papers. But when she went in she was not only disappointed but also frightened: the papers were bills, electricity, gas, phone, all unpaid and organized chronologically. No one had noticed this? No one knew there was a man living in these conditions in a middle-class neighborhood? There were probably papers of other kinds among the unpaid bills, but Paula had to hurry and she turned to look over the books. They were all big, heavy medical books from the seventies, with satiny pages interspersed with glossy illustrations. The first one she flipped through didn't have any marks, but the second one did; it was an anatomy book, and on the pages that described the feminine reproductive system someone had used a green ballpoint pen to draw an enormous cock with spikes on the glans, and, in the uterus, a baby with large, glaucous eyes who wasn't sucking his thumb, he was licking it with a lascivious gesture that made her say aloud: "What *is* this?" When she heard the key in the front door she threw the book to the floor; she felt a sudden wetness in her underwear and pants and she ran to the courtyard, climbed desperately onto the tank—*I'll fall, I'll fall, my hands are sweaty, my blood pressure is low*—and with fear-induced speed, she made it to her own terrace. She went running down the stairs and locked the courtyard door, though she didn't think that would stop the man who would surely be coming after her, because he must have heard her, because she had left the door to his fetid pantry open, because she had seen his drawings. What other drawings were there? What did those walls say? And the boy? Was it a boy? Or had it been the man himself? Did he sometimes like to chain himself up in the courtyard? It could be him; with distance and the influence of her own history with children, maybe he had seemed smaller than he really was. A relief, to think that the boy didn't exist. But the relief didn't protect her. Maybe the crazy man wasn't dangerous; maybe he wouldn't care that she'd broken into his house.

But Paula didn't think so. She was remembering things seen out of the corner of her eye. Something on the couch that looked like a wig. Some words on the wall that were in a language she didn't know, or were in an invented language, or were simply letters grouped senselessly. How all the plants in the yard were dried up, but the earth was damp as if someone kept watering them, as if someone refused to accept the fact that they were dead.

For the first time, she hated Miguel unequivocally. For leaving her alone, for judging her, for being a coward, for running away at the first real problem. For running to his mommy! She called him. Asshole.

"He's not here," her mother-in-law told her. "Are you all right, dear?"

"No, I'm shitty."

Silence.

"Call him on his cell phone, darling, you're going to be fine, don't you worry."

She hung up. Miguel's cell phone had been turned off for hours. In situations like this she missed her father, a complicated and not very affectionate man, but clear and decisive, a man who would never have gotten scared or angry over such a small thing. She remembered how he had taken care of her mother, driven mad by a brain tumor that eventually killed her. When he'd heard her screams not a muscle in his face had moved, but he hadn't told her that everything was fine. Because everything wasn't fine and it was stupid to deny it.

Like now: something bad was going to happen and it was stupid to deny it.

She tried to call his phone one more time, but it was still off or out of range. Then she heard Elly, growling in anger and then meowing wildly. The cat's cries were coming from the bedroom. Paula ran.

A boy was sitting on the bed with Elly on his lap. He looked at her, and his glaucous eyes were crisscrossed with red veins and his eyelids were gray and greasy like sardines. He stank, too. His stench filled the room. He was bald and so skinny it was amazing he was alive. He was stroking the cat brutally, blindly, with a hand that was too big for his body. His other hand was around Elly's neck.

"Let go of her!" screamed Paula.

It was the boy from the neighbor's house. He had marks from the chain on his ankle; in some places they were bleeding and in others they oozed with infection. When he heard her voice the boy smiled, and she saw his teeth. They'd been filed into triangular shapes, like arrowheads, or like a saw. The boy brought the cat to his mouth with a lightning-fast motion and clamped the saw into her belly. Elly yowled and Paula saw the agony in her eyes while the boy's teeth delved farther into her stomach. He buried his face, nose and all, in her guts, he inhaled inside the cat, who died quickly, looking at her owner with angry and surprised eyes. Paula didn't run. She didn't do anything while the boy devoured the animal's soft parts, until his teeth hit her spine and he tossed the cadaver into a corner.

"Why?" Paula asked him. "What are you?"

But the boy didn't understand her. He stood up on legs of pure bone, his sex disproportionately large, his face covered in blood, in guts and Elly's silky fur. He seemed to be looking for something on the bed; when he found it, he lifted it up toward the ceiling lamp, as if he wanted Paula to see the object clearly.

He had her front door keys. The boy made them jangle and he laughed and his laughter was accompanied by a bloody belch. Paula wanted to run, but her legs were heavy as if in a nightmare. Her body refused to turn around; something was holding her there in the bedroom doorway. But she wasn't dreaming. You don't feel pain in dreams.

# Under the Black Water

The cop came in with his head high and proud, his wrists free of cuffs, wearing the ironic smile she knew so well; he oozed impunity and contempt. She'd seen many like him. She had managed to convict far too few.

"Have a seat, Officer," she told him.

The district attorney's office was on the first floor and her window looked out onto nothing, just a hollow between buildings. She'd been asking for a change in office and jurisdiction for a long time. She hated the darkness of that hundred-year-old building, and hated even more that her cases came from the impoverished slums on the city's south side, cases where crime was always mixed with hardship.

The cop sat down, and she reluctantly asked her secretary to bring two cups of coffee.

"You know why you're here. You also know you are under no obligation to tell me anything. Why didn't you bring your lawyer?"

"I know how to defend myself. And anyway, I'm innocent."

The district attorney sighed and toyed with her ring. How many times had she witnessed this exact scene? How many times had a cop like this one denied, to her face and against all evidence, that he had murdered a poor teenager? Because that was what the cops did in the southern slums, much more than protect people: they killed teenagers, sometimes out of cruelty, other times because the kids refused to "work" for them—to steal for them or sell the drugs the police seized. Or for betraying them. The reasons for killing poor kids were many and despicable.

"Officer, we have your voice on tape. Would you like to hear the recording?"

"I don't say anything on that tape."

"You don't say anything. Let's have a listen, then."

She had the audio file on her computer, and she opened it. The cop's voice came through the speakers: "Problem solved. They learned to swim."

The cop snorted. "What does that prove?" he asked.

"By the time stamp as well as your words, it proves that you at least knew that two young men had been thrown into the Ricachuelo."

Pinat had been investigating the case for two months. After bribing police to talk, after threats and afternoons of rage brought on by the incompetence of the judge and the DAs who'd come before her, she had put together a version of events on which the few final and formally obtained statements agreed: Emanuel López and Yamil Corvalán, both fifteen, had gone dancing in Constitución and were returning home to Villa Moreno, a slum on the banks of the Riachuelo. They went on foot because they didn't have money for the bus. They were intercepted by two cops from the thirty-fourth precinct who accused them of trying to rob a kiosk; Yamil had a knife on him, but that attempted robbery was never confirmed, since there was no police report. The cops were drunk. They beat the teens almost unconscious on the riverbank. Next, they kicked them up the cement stairs to the lookout on the bridge over the river, then pushed them into the water. "Problem solved, they learned to swim," were the words that Officer Cuesta, the accused man who was now in her office, had said over the official radio. The idiot hadn't had the conversation erased; all her years as DA had also accustomed her to that, to the impossible combination of brutality and stupidity she encountered in the cops she dealt with.

Yamil Corvalán's body washed up a kilometer down from the bridge. At that point the Riachuelo has almost no current; it is calm and dead, with its oil and plastic scraps and heavy chemicals, the city's great garbage can. The autopsy established that the boy had tried to swim through the black grease. He had drowned when his arms couldn't move anymore. The police had tried for months to sustain the fiction that the teenager's death was accidental, but a woman had heard his screams that night: "Please, please! Help! They pushed me in! I'm drowning!" the boy shouted. The woman hadn't tried to help him. She knew it was impossible to get him out of the water except with a boat, and she didn't have a boat. None of the neighbors did.

Emanuel's body hadn't surfaced. But his parents confirmed he had gone out with Yamil that night. And his running shoes had washed ashore, unmistakable because they were an expensive, imported brand. He'd surely stolen them, and he'd worn them that night to impress the girls at the dance club. His mother had recognized them immediately. She also said that Officers Cuesta and Suárez had been harassing her son, though she didn't know why. The DA had questioned her in that very office the week the teenagers had disappeared. The woman had cried; she'd cried and said that her son was a good boy although yes, sometimes he stole and every once in a while he did drugs, but that was because his father had left them and they were very poor and the boy wanted things, shoes and an iPhone and all the stuff he saw on TV. And he didn't deserve to die like that, drowned because some cops wanted to laugh at him, to laugh while he tried to swim in the polluted water.

No, of course he didn't deserve it, she'd told the woman.

"Ma'am, I did not throw anyone in the river." The cop leaned back in his chair. "And that's all I'm saying."

"As you wish. This was your chance to make a deal that could, maybe, lessen your sentence. We need to know where that body is, and if you give us that information, who knows, maybe you could go to a smaller jail or to the evangelist cell block. You know the evangelists would go easier on you."

The cop laughed. He was laughing at her, and he was laughing at the dead boys.

"You think they're gonna give me much time? For this?"

"I'm going to try to have you locked up for good."

The DA was about to lose her cool. She squeezed her hands into fists. She looked into the cop's eyes for a moment, and then he said very clearly, in a different, more serious voice, without a trace of irony:

"If only that whole slum would go up in flames. Or every last one of those people would drown. You don't know what goes on there. You. You have no idea."

---

SHE DID HAVE SOME IDEA. Marina Pinat had been DA for eight years. She'd visited the Villa Moreno slum several times even though it wasn't required by her job—she could investigate from her desk like all her colleagues did, but she preferred to meet the people she read about in the files. Just months before, her investigation had helped a group of families win a case against a nearby tannery that had been dumping chromium and other toxic waste into the water for decades. It had been an extensive and complex civil suit she'd spent years working on. There were families who lived by the water and drank it, and though the mothers boiled it to try to get the poison out, their children got sick, consumed by cancer in three months, with horrible skin eruptions that ate away at their legs and arms. And some of them had been born with deformities. Extra arms (sometimes up to four), noses wide like felines, eyes blind and set close to their temples. She didn't remember the name that the doctors, somewhat confused, had given that birth defect. She remembered one of them had called it "mutation."

During that investigation she had met the slum's cleric, Father Francisco, a young parish priest who didn't even wear the white collar. No one came to church, he'd told her. He ran a soup kitchen for the children of the poorest families and he helped where he could, but he'd given up on any kind of pastoral work. There weren't many faithful left, just a few old women. Most of the slum's inhabitants were devotees of Afro-Brazilian cults, or they had adopted their own doctrines, worshipping personal saints like George or Expeditus, setting up shrines to them on corners. "It's not bad," he said, but he didn't say mass anymore except when that handful of old women asked him to. It had seemed to Marina that, behind the smile, the beard, and the long hair—his look of a militant revolutionary from the seventies—the young and well-meaning priest was tired, burdened with a dark desperation.

When the cop left and slammed the door behind him, the DA's secretary waited a few minutes before knocking on the door and announcing that someone else was waiting to see her.

"Not today, hon," said Pinat. She'd been left exhausted and furious, as always when she had to talk with cops.

The secretary shook his head and his eyes implored her.

"Please, Marina, see her. You don't know . . . "

"OK, OK. But this is the last one."

The secretary nodded and thanked her with a look. Marina was already thinking about what to make for dinner that night, or if she felt like going out to a restaurant. Her car was at the mechanic's but she could use the bike; the nights were cool and beautiful that time of year. She wanted to get out of the office, invite a friend out for a beer. She wanted that day to be over and the investigation too, and for the boy's body to finally turn up once and for all.

While she was putting her keys, cigarettes, and some papers into her purse so she could leave quickly, a pregnant teenager came into her office; she was horribly skinny and didn't want to give her name. Marina took a Coca-Cola from the small refrigerator she had under her desk and told her, "I'm listening."

"Emanuel is in Villa Moreno," said the girl between long gulps of soda.

"How far along are you?" Marina asked, indicating the girl's belly.

"I dunno."

Of course she didn't know. Marina calculated the pregnancy was some six months along. The girl's fingertips were burned, stained with the chemical yellow of the crack pipe. The baby, if it was born alive, would be sick, deformed, or addicted.

"How do you know Emanuel?"

"We all know him. Everyone in Moreno knows his family. I went to his funeral. Emanuel used to be kind of my sister's boyfriend."

"And your sister, where is she? Did she recognize him too?"

"No, my sister doesn't live there anymore."

"I'll see. Go on."

"People say Emanuel came out of the water."

"The night they threw him in?"

"No. That's why I'm here. He came out a couple of weeks ago. He's only been back a little while."

Marina felt a shiver. The girl had an addict's dilated pupils, and in the half-light of the office, her eyes looked completely black, like a carrion insect's.

"What do you mean he came back? Did he go somewhere?"

The girl looked at her like she was stupid and her voice became thicker as she held back laughter.

"No! He didn't *go* anywhere. He came back from the water. He was in the water the whole time."

"You're lying."

"No. I came to tell you because you need to know. Emanuel wants to meet you."

She tried not to focus on the way the girl was moving her fingers, stained from the toxic pipe, interweaving them as if they didn't have joints or were extraordinarily soft. Could she be one of the deformed children, the ones with birth defects from the polluted water? No, she was too old. But when had the mutations started? Anything was possible.

"And where is Emanuel now?"

"He's holed up in one of the houses back behind the tracks. He lives there with his friends. Are you going to give me money now? They told me you'd give me money."

Marina kept her in the office a while longer, but she couldn't get much more out of the girl. Emanuel López had come out of the Riachuelo, she said. People had seen him walking through the slum's labyrinthine alleys, and some of them had run away, scared to death when their paths crossed his. They said he walked slowly, and he stank. His mother hadn't wanted to take him in. That part surprised Marina. And he'd gone into one of the vacant houses at the far end of Villa Moreno, past the abandoned train tracks. The girl yanked the bill from Marina's hands when she finally paid her for her testimony. The DA had found her greed reassuring. She thought the girl was lying. Surely some cop friend of the murderers had sent her—or they'd sent her themselves; they were only on house arrest and they certainly didn't comply with it. If one of the boys turned out to be alive, the whole case could collapse. The accused cops had told a lot of their colleagues about how they tortured young thieves by making them "swim" in the Riachuelo. Some of those colleagues had talked, after months of negotiation and outlays of large sums of money to pay for the information. The crime was corroborated, but a dead man who turned out to be alive was one crime less, and it would cast a shadow of doubt over the entire investigation.

That night, Marina was uneasy when she went back to her apartment after a quick and not very stimulating dinner at a new restaurant that had good reviews but terrible service. Her common sense told her that the pregnant girl was only after money, but there was something in her story that sounded strangely real, like a living nightmare. She slept badly, thinking of the dead-but-alive boy's hand touching the shore, the ghost swimmer who returned months after he was murdered. She dreamed that when the boy emerged from the water and shook off the muck, the fingers fell off his hands. She woke up smelling the stench of dead meat, consumed with a horrible fear of finding those swollen, infected fingers between her sheets.

She waited until dawn to try to call someone in Moreno: Emanuel's mother, or Father Francisco. No answer. That wasn't strange; cell phone reception was poor in the city and even worse in the slum. She got alarmed when no one answered the phone in the priest's soup kitchen or in the first-aid clinic. Now that was odd: those places had landlines. Could they have gone out in the last storm?

She kept trying to get in touch with someone all day, unsuccessfully. She canceled everything that afternoon—she told her secretary that her head hurt and she was going to spend the time reading files, and he, ever obedient, had suspended all of her meetings and hearings. That night, as she cooked spaghetti for dinner, she decided that the very next day she would go to Villa Moreno.

NOT MUCH HAD CHANGED since her last time on that southern edge of the city, on the desolate street that led to Moreno Bridge. Out there, Buenos Aires gradually frayed into abandoned storefronts, house windows bricked up to keep squatters out, rusted signs crowning buildings from the seventies. There were still some clothing stores, sketchy butcher shops, and the church, which she remembered being shuttered and still was, she saw now from the taxi; there was, though, a new chain on the door for extra security. This street, she knew, was the dead zone, the emptiest place in the neighborhood. Beyond those run-down façades, which served as a warning, lived the city's poor. Along both of the Riachuelo's banks, thousands of people had used the empty land to build their houses, which ranged from precarious tin shacks to quite decent brick-and-cement apartment buildings. From the bridge you could see the extent of the slum; it stretched out along the black, calm river, fading from sight where there was a bend in the water and it disappeared into the distance among the smokestacks of abandoned factories. People had been talking for years about cleaning up the Riachuelo, that branch of the Rio de la Plata that wended into the city and then moved off southward. For a century it had been the chosen site for dumping all kinds of waste, but especially the offal from cows. Every time Marina got close to the Riachuelo she remembered the stories she'd heard from her father, who for a very short time had been a laborer on the river barges. He told of how they'd dumped everything overboard: the scraps of meat and bone, the muck the animals brought from the country, the shit, the gummed-up grass. "The water turned red," he said. "People were afraid of it."

He also explained to her that the Riachuelo's deep and rotten stench, which with the right wind and the city's constant humidity could hang in the air for days, was caused by the lack of oxygen in the water. Anoxia, he'd told her. "The organic material consumes the oxygen in the liquid," he said with his pompous chemistry teacher's gestures. She'd never understood the formulas, which her father found simple and thrilling, but she never forgot that the black river along the city's edge was basically dead, decomposing: it couldn't breathe. It was the most polluted river in the world, experts affirmed. Maybe there was one with the same degree of toxicity in China, the only place that could possibly compare. But China was the most industrialized country in the world; Argentina had taken the river winding around its capital, which could have made for a beautiful day trip, and polluted it almost arbitrarily, practically for the fun of it.

The fact that the crowded hovels of Villa Moreno had been built along the banks of that river depressed Marina. Only truly desperate people went to live there, beside that dangerous and deliberate putrescence.

"This is as far as I go, ma'am."

The driver's voice startled her.

"Where I'm going is three hundred meters farther on," she answered, distant and dry, the tone of voice she used to address lawyers and police officers.

The man shook his head no and turned the car's motor off.

"You can't force me to go into the Villa. I'm asking you to get out here. Are you going in alone?"

The driver sounded frightened, genuinely frightened. She told him yes. Certainly, she'd tried to convince the dead boys' lawyer to come with her, but he had plans he couldn't change. "You're crazy, Marina," he'd told her. "I'll go with you tomorrow, but today I can't." But she'd been single-minded. And what was she worried about, after all? She'd gone to Moreno several times before. It was the middle of the day. A lot of people knew her; no one would touch her.

She threatened to complain about the driver's behavior to the owners of the taxi service; what a scandal to leave a judiciary official on foot in that area. She couldn't move the man an inch, which was the reaction she expected. No one went near the slum around Moreno Bridge unless it was unavoidable. It was a dangerous place. She herself had left behind her little tailored suits she always wore in the office and in court, opting instead for jeans, a dark shirt, and nothing in her pockets except money to get home and her telephone, both so she could communicate with her contacts in the Villa and so she'd have something valuable to hand over if she was mugged. And of course her gun, which she had a license to use, was discreetly hidden under her shirt. Not so hidden, though, that the outline of its butt and barrel couldn't be seen on her back.

She could enter the Villa by walking down the embankment to the left of the bridge alongside an abandoned building that, strangely, no one had decided to occupy. It was rotting away, corroded by damp, sporting ancient signs advertising massages, tarot readings, accountants, loans. But first she decided to go up onto the bridge; she wanted to see and touch the last place Emanuel and Yamil had seen before they were murdered by police.

The cement stairs were dirty and reeked of urine and rotten food, but she headed up them at a trot. At forty years old, Marina Pinat was in good shape; she went jogging every morning and the court employees whispered that she was "well-preserved" for her age. She detested those murmurings; she wasn't flattered, they offended her. She didn't want to be beautiful, she wanted to be strong and razor sharp.

She reached the platform the boys had been thrown from. She looked down at the stagnant black river and couldn't imagine falling from up there toward that still water, couldn't fathom how the drivers of the cars passing intermittently behind her hadn't seen a thing.

SHE LEFT THE BRIDGE and walked down the embankment by the abandoned building. As soon as she set foot on the street that led into the Villa, she was disconcerted by the silence. It was terribly quiet. That silence was impossible. The neighborhood—any slum, even this one, where only the most idealistic or naïve social workers dared to tread, even in this dangerous and shunned place—should have been full of varied and pleasant sounds. That was how it always was. The different rhythms of music mixing together: the slow, sensual *cumbia villera*; that shrill mix of reggae with a Caribbean beat; the always-present *cumbia santafesina*, with its romantic and sometimes violent lyrics; the motorcycles with their exhaust pipes cut, roaring as they got going; all the people who came and bought and walked and talked. The sizzling grills with their chorizos and chickens, their skewers of meat. The slums always teemed with people, with running kids, with teenagers in baseball caps drinking beers with dogs.

The Moreno Bridge slum, however, was now as dead and silent as the water in the Riachuelo.

As she took her phone from her back pocket, she had the feeling she was being watched from the alleyways that were darkened by electrical wires and clothes drying on lines. All the blinds were drawn, at least along that street that edged the water. It had rained, and she tried not to step in the puddles so she wouldn't get muddy as she walked—she could never stand still when she talked on the phone.

Father Francisco didn't answer. Nor did Emanuel's mother. She thought she could find the small church without a guide; she remembered the way. It was near the entrance to the Villa, like most parish churches. In the short walk there she was surprised at the utter absence of shrines to popular saints—the Gauchito Gils, the Yemojas, even some virgins who usually had a few offerings. She recognized a small yellow-painted house on one of the villa's corners and was comforted to know she wasn't lost. But before she turned that corner, she heard faint steps that squelched—someone was running behind her. She turned around. It was one of the deformed children. She realized it immediately—how could she not? Over time, the face that was ugly on babies had become more horrible: the very wide nose, like a cat's, the eyes wide apart, close to the temples. He opened his mouth, perhaps to call her; he had no teeth.

His body was eight or ten years old, and he didn't have a single tooth.

The boy came up to her, and when he was beside her she could see how the rest of his defects had developed; the fingers had suckers and were thin like squid tails (or were they legs? She never knew what to call them). The boy didn't stop when he reached her. He kept walking toward the church as if guiding her.

The church looked deserted. It had always been a modest house, painted white, and the only indication it was a religious building had been the metal cross on the roof. It was still there, but now it was painted yellow, and someone had decorated it with a crown of yellow and white flowers; from afar they looked like daisies. But the walls of the church were no longer clean. They were covered in graffiti. From up close Marina could see that they were letters, but they didn't form words: YAINGNGA-

HYOGSOTHOTHHEELGEBFAITHRODOG. The order of the letters, she noticed, was always the same, but it still made no sense to her. The deformed boy opened the church door; Marina shifted her gun to her side and went in.

The building was no longer a church. It had never had wooden pews or a formal altar, just chairs facing a table where Father Francisco gave his sporadic masses. But now it was completely empty, the walls covered in graffiti that copied the letters outside: YAINGNGAHYOGSOTHOTHHEELGEBFAITHRODOG. The crucifix had disappeared, as had the images of the sacred heart of Jesus and Our Lady of Luján.

In place of the altar there was a wooden pole stuck into a common metal flowerpot. And impaled on the pole was a cow's head. The idol—because that's what it was, Marina realized—had to have been recently made, because there was no smell of rotting meat in the church. The head was fresh.

"You shouldn't have come," she heard the priest say. He had entered the building behind her. When she saw him she was even more convinced that something was horribly wrong. The priest was emaciated and dirty, his beard was overgrown and his hair was so greasy it looked wet. But the most startling thing was that he was drunk, and the stench of alcohol oozed from his pores. When he came into the church it was as if he'd poured a bottle of whiskey over the filthy floor.

"You shouldn't have come," he repeated, and then he slipped. Marina noticed the trailed drops of fresh blood that led from the door to the cow's head.

"What is this, Francisco?"

It took the priest a while to answer. But the deformed child, who had stayed in a corner of what had once been the church, said:

"In his house, the dead man waits dreaming."

"That's all these stupid shits know how to say!" the priest cried, and Marina, who had reached out her arm to help him up from the floor, recoiled. "Filthy, defiled retards! So they sent that *whore* they got *pregnant* to talk to you, and that was all it took to get you to come? I didn't think you were that stupid."

In the distance, Marina heard drums. The *murga,* she thought, relieved. It was February. Of course. That was it. The people had gone to practice the *murga* for carnival, or maybe they were already celebrating in the soccer field over by the train tracks.

"He's holed up in one of the houses back behind the tracks. He lives there, with his friends." *But how did the priest know about the pregnant girl?*

It was the *murga*, she was sure. The Villa had a traditional troupe and they always celebrated carnival. It was a little early, but it was possible. And the cow's head must be a gift from one of the neighborhood drug dealers, meant to intimidate. They hated Father Francisco because he reported them to the police or tried to rehabilitate the addicted kids, which meant taking away their customers and employees.

"You have to get out of here, Francisco," she told him.

The priest laughed.

"I tried. I tried! But there's no getting out. You're not going to get out either. That boy woke up the thing sleeping under the water. Don't you hear them? The cult of the dead? Don't you hear the drums?"

"It's carnival."

"Carnival? Does that sound like carnival to you?"

"You're drunk. How did you know about the pregnant girl?"

"That's no carnival."

The priest stood up and tried to light a cigarette.

"You know, for years I thought that rotten river was a sign of our ineptitude. How we never think about the future. Sure, we'll just toss all the muck in here, let the river wash it away! We never think about the consequences. A country full of incompetents. But now I see things differently, Marina. Those people *were* being responsible when they polluted that river. They were covering something up, something they didn't want to let out, and they buried it under layers and layers of oil and mud! They even clogged the river with boats! Just left them there, deadlocked!"

"What are you talking about?"

"Don't play dumb. You were never stupid. The police started throwing people in there because *they* are stupid. And most of the people they threw in died, but some of them found it. Do you know the kind of foulness that reaches us here? The shit from all the houses, all the filth from the sewers, everything! Layers and layers of filth to keep it dead or asleep. It's the same thing, I believe sleep and death are the same thing. And it worked, until people started to do the unthinkable: they swam under the black water. And they woke the thing up. Do you know what *Emanuel* means? It means 'God is with us.' The problem is, what God are we talking about?"

"You're talking bullshit, that's the problem. Let's go, I'm getting you out of here."

The priest started to rub his eyes so hard Marina was afraid he would tear his corneas. The blind, deformed child had turned around and now had his back to them, his forehead against the wall.

"They set him on me to guard me. He's their son."

Marina tried to piece together what was really happening: the priest, hounded by those who hated him in the Villa, had gone crazy. The deformed child, who'd surely been abandoned by his family, followed him everywhere because he had no one else. The neighborhood people had taken their music and their barbecues to the carnival festivities. It was all frightening, but it wasn't impossible. There was no dead boy walking around, there was no death cult.

*But why were there no religious images? And why had the priest talked about Emanuel when she hadn't even asked?*

It doesn't matter, we're leaving, thought Marina, and she grabbed the priest's arm so he could lean on her to walk, since he was too drunk to do it alone. That was a mistake. She had no time to react; the priest was drunk, but his movement when he grabbed her gun was surprisingly fast and precise. She couldn't even fight back, nor did she see that the deformed child had turned around and started screaming mutely. His mouth was open and he screamed without a sound.

The priest pointed the gun at her. She looked around, her heart pummeling her ribs, her mouth dry. She couldn't escape; he was drunk, he might miss, but it wasn't likely in such a small space. She started to plead, but he interrupted her.

"I don't want to kill you. I want to thank you."

And then he wasn't pointing the gun at her. He lowered it and then quickly raised it again, put it in his mouth, and fired.

The shot left Marina deaf. The priest's brains now covered part of the nonsense letters, and the boy repeated: "In his house, the dead man waits dreaming." He had trouble with the *r* sound, though, and he pronounced it "dweaming." Marina didn't try to help the priest; there was no chance he'd survived the shot.

She took the gun from his hand and couldn't help thinking that her prints were everywhere, that she could be accused of killing him. Shitty priest, shitty slum, why was she even there? To prove what, and to whom? The gun was trembling in her hand, now covered in blood. She didn't know how she was going to go home with her hands all bloodied. She had to find clean water.

When she emerged from the church she realized she was crying, and that the Villa wasn't empty anymore. Her deafness after the gunshot had made her think the drums were still far away, but she was wrong. The *murga* was passing right in front of the church. Only it was clear now that it wasn't a *murga*. It was a procession. A line of people playing the same loud snare drums as in the *murga*, led by deformed children with their skinny arms and mollusk fingers, followed by women, most of them fat, their bodies disfigured by a diet based on carbs. There were some men, just a few, and Marina recognized among them some policemen she knew; she even thought she recognized Súarez, with his dark hair slicked back and wearing his uniform, violating his house arrest.

After them came the idol, which they were carrying on a bed. That was what it was: a bed, complete with a mattress. Marina couldn't see the figure clearly; it was lying down. It was human-sized. She had once seen something similar during Holy Week, effigies of Jesus just taken down from the cross, blood on white cloth, something between a bed and a coffin.

She moved closer to the procession, though everything told her she should run in the opposite direction. She wanted to see what was lying on the bed.

*The dead man waits dreaming.*

Among the people walking quietly, the only sound came from the drums. She tried to move closer to the idol, craning her neck, but the bed was very high, inexplicably high. A woman pushed her when she tried to get too close and Marina recognized her; it was Emanuel's mother. She tried to stop her but the woman murmured something about the barges and the dark depths of the water, where the house was, and she pushed Marina away from her with a head butt right when the people in the procession began to shout "yo, yo, yo," and the thing they were carrying on the bed moved a little, enough for one of its gray arms to fall over the side of the bed. It was like the arm of a very sick person, and Marina remembered the fingers in her dream, the fingers falling from the rotten hand, and only then did she start running away with her gun drawn. While she ran she prayed in a low voice like she hadn't done since she was a child. She ran between the precarious houses, through labyrinthine alleys, searching for the embankment, the shore, trying to ignore the fact that the black water seemed agitated, because it couldn't be, because that water didn't breathe, the water was dead, it couldn't kiss the banks with waves, it couldn't be ruffled by the wind, it couldn't have those eddies or the current or that swelling, how could there be a swelling when the water was stagnant? Marina ran toward the bridge and didn't look back and she covered her ears with her bloody hands to block out the noise of the drums.

# Green Red Orange

It's been almost two years since he became a green or red or orange dot on my screen. I never see him, he won't let me. He won't let anyone else, either. Every once in a long while he'll talk, at least with me, but he doesn't turn on his camera so I don't know if he still has long hair and the thinness of a bird. He looked like a bird the last time I saw him, crouched down on the bed, his hands too large and his nails long.

Before he locked his bedroom door from inside, he'd had two weeks of so-called brain shivers. They're a common side effect when you stop taking antidepressants, and they feel like gentle electrical discharges inside your head. He described them like the painful cramp you feel when you hit your elbow. I never really believed he felt them. I used to visit him in his dark room and listen to him talk about that and twenty other side effects, and it was like he was reciting from a medical book. I knew a lot of people who took or had taken antidepressants and none of their brains short-circuited; they just gained weight or had weird dreams or slept too much.

"You always have to be so special," I told him one afternoon, and he covered his eyes with his arm. I remember I thought how sick I was of him and his whole soap opera. That day I also remembered the time when, after drinking half a bottle of wine, I'd pulled down his pants and his underwear and I licked and caressed his dick. Then, surprised and a little angry, I wrapped my hand around it and started to stroke it with the rhythm I knew was irresistible until he put a hand on my head and said, "It's not going to work." I left, furious, after dumping the rest of the wine over his sheets, and I didn't go see him again for a week. We never talked about what had happened, and I never saw any red stains. I wasn't in love with him anymore, I'd just wanted to show him that he was exaggerating that sadness of his for no reason. It was no use, though, just like it was no use getting angry or accusing him of lying.

When he locked himself in for good—his room had its own bathroom, with a shower—his mother thought he was going to kill himself and she called me in tears to ask me to come try and stop him. Of course at the time, neither she nor I knew his seclusion would be permanent. I talked to him through the door, I knocked, I called him on the phone. His psychiatrist did the same. I thought that in a few days he would open the door and start moping around the house as usual. I was wrong, and two years later I wait for him every night—green red orange—and I get scared when he's gray for too many days. He doesn't use his name, Marco. He just goes by M.

SAD PEOPLE ARE MERCILESS. Marco lives in his mother's house and she cooks his four daily meals, and now she leaves them outside his closed door on a tray. She started doing that because he told her to, by text message. He also told her: *Don't wait for me or try to see me.* She didn't listen, of course. She waited for hours, but he has a freakish resolve. Marco can handle hunger. His mother tried letting him go for days without eating. She also tried, on the psychiatrist's advice, cutting off his Internet service. Marco managed to steal the neighbor's Wi-Fi until his mother felt guilty and got the connection back for him. He doesn't thank her, or ask her for anything. His mother invites me to their house sometimes but I almost never accept—I can't stand the thought of him listening to our conversation from his room. We go to a café near my apartment and all the conversations are the same. What can she do, he refuses treatment, she can't kick him out, he's her son, she feels guilty even though nothing ever happened to Marco, neither she nor her husband abused him, he was never molested, there are photos of seaside vacations and the world's sweetest boy who dressed up as Batman and collected soccer cards in an album and liked sports. I always tell her that Marco is sick and it's no one's fault, it's his brain, it's chemical, it's genetic. "If he had cancer," I tell her, "you wouldn't think it's your fault. It isn't your fault he's depressed."

She asks if he talks to me. I tell her the truth: yes, or more like he chats—because he talks less and less, he's disappearing into the Internet; Marco is letters that titillate, and sometimes he just disappears without waiting for an answer—but that he never tells me what's going on, what he's feeling, what he wants. It's horribly different from how it was before the lock-in. Before, he talked obsessively about his therapy, his pills, his problems concentrating; about when he'd stopped studying because he couldn't remember anything of what he read; about his migraines; about not feeling hungry. Now, he talks about whatever he wants. In general, about the deep web and the Red Room and Japanese ghosts. But I don't tell his mother that part. I lie and say we talk about books and movies that he watches and reads online. "Ah," she breathes, "I can't cut off his Internet then, it's the only thing that connects him to life."

She says stuff like that, *connect to life, forge ahead, we have to be strong*: she's a stupid woman. I always ask her why she thinks I'll be able to get Marco out of his room—because she often asks me to knock on the door and beg. Sometimes I do it, and later on at night he finds me on chat and writes: *Don't be dumb. Just ignore her.*

"Why do you think I can get him out?" I ask her, and she pours milk into her coffee until it's ruined, turned into a hot cream. "The last time I saw him happy was when you two were together," she says, and she lowers her head. She uses bad-quality dye and the tips of her hair are always too light, and the roots gray. What she says is not true; Marco and I lived in silence and impotence. I'd ask him, "What's wrong with you?" and he'd reply that nothing was wrong, or he'd sit in bed and scream that he was a soulless shell. "The soap opera" was my name for those tantrums that always ended in crying fits and drunken binges. Maybe he told his mother we were happy. Maybe she simply decided to believe it. Maybe he decided that his sadness was going to be my companion forever, for as long as he wanted, because sad people are merciless.

"TODAY I READ AN ARTICLE ABOUT PEOPLE LIKE YOU," I wrote to him one morning at dawn. "You're a *hikikomori*. You know about them, right? They're Japanese people who lock themselves in their rooms and their families support them. They don't have any mental problems, it's just that things are unbearable for them: the pressure of university, having a social life, those kinds of things. Their parents never kick them out. It's an epidemic in Japan. It almost doesn't exist in other countries. Sometimes they come out, especially at night, alone. To find food, for example. They don't make their mothers cook for them like you do."

"I come out sometimes," he answered.

I hesitated before answering.

"When?"

"When my mother goes to work. Or early in the morning. She doesn't hear me, she takes sleeping pills."

"I don't believe you."

"You know the best thing about the Japanese? They classify ghosts."

"Tell me what time you come out and we'll meet."

"The ghosts of children are called *zashiki-warashi* and supposedly they aren't evil. The evil ones are the ghosts of women. They have a lot of spirits that are girls cut in half, for example. They drag themselves over the floor, they're just torsos, and if you catch sight of them they kill you. There's a kind of mother ghost called *ubume,* and they're women who died in childbirth. They steal children or bring them candy. They also classify the ghosts of people who died at sea."

"Tell me what time you come out and I'll visit you."

"I was lying about coming out."

I angrily closed the chat window, though he didn't disconnect, he stayed green. *I am not going to go stand in front of his house for the six hours his mother is at work,* I swore to myself, and I kept my promise.

---

INTERNET IN THE NINETIES was a white cable that went from my computer to the phone jack on the other side of the house. My Internet friends felt real, and I got anxious when the connection or the electricity went out and I couldn't meet them to talk about symbolism, glam rock, David Bowie, Iggy Pop, Manic Street Preachers, English occultists, Latin American dictatorships. One of my friends was locked in, I remember. She was Swedish, and her English was perfect—I had almost no Argentine friends online. She had a social phobia, she said. I can't recover her emails; they're backed up on an old computer that won't turn on. I deleted the account years ago. She used to send me documentaries on VHS and CDs that were impossible to get outside Europe. Back then I didn't wonder how she managed to get to the post office since she supposedly couldn't go out. Maybe she was lying. But the packages came from Sweden: she wasn't lying about where she was. I still have the stamps, although the videotapes got moldy and the CDs stopped working and she in turn disappeared forever, a ghost of the net, and I can't look for her because I don't remember her name. I remember other names. Rhias, for example, from Portland, fan of the decadent movement and of superheroes. We had a kind of romance, and she sent me poems by Anne Sexton. Heather, from England, who still exists and who, she says, will always be grateful to me for introducing her to Johnny Thunders. Keeper, who fell in love with young boys. Another girl who wrote beautiful poems that I can't remember either, except for the occasional bad line. "My blue someone," for example, *mi alguien triste.* Marco offered to get them all back for me. All my lost friends. He says being locked in turned him into a hacker. But I'd rather forget them because forgetting people you only knew in words is odd; when they existed they were more intense than people in real life, and now they're more distant than strangers. Plus, I'm a little scared of them. I found Rhias on Facebook. She accepted my friend request and I wrote to her happily, but she never answered and we never spoke again. I think she doesn't remember me or she only remembers me a little, vaguely, as if she'd met me in a dream.

MARCO NEVER SCARES ME except when he talks about the deep web. He says he needs to learn about it. That's how he puts it: it's a need. The deep web is all the sites that aren't indexed in search engines. It's much bigger than the superficial web that we all use. Five thousand times bigger. I don't understand it and I get bored when he explains how to find it, but he assures me it's not that hard. "What's there?" I ask him.

"They sell drugs, weapons, sex," he tells me. "I'm not interested in most of it," he says, "but there are some things I want to see. Like the Red Room. It's a chat room you pay to get into. People talk about a tortured girl whose breasts are beaten to a pulp by a thin black man who kicks them. Then they rape her until they kill her. The video of the torture is for sale, and so is an archive of her screams that don't sound like anything human and are unforgettable. And I want to learn about the RRC," he says.

"What's that?" I ask.

"The Real Rape Community. They have no rules. They starve kids to death. They force them to have sex with animals. They strangle them and of course, they rape them. It's the most perverse place on the web, or it was. Now there's a place for sex with corpses."

"Having sex with children is much worse than with corpses," I write.

"Sure," replies Marco.

"I wonder where they get the kids' corpses."

"Anywhere. I don't know why you all think that kids are cared for and loved."

"Did someone do something to you when you were little?"

"Never. You always ask me the same thing, you always want explanations."

"I think this whole thing about the deep web is a lie. Who is 'you all'?"

"It's not a lie, there are articles in serious newspapers. Look them up. They mostly talk about sites where you can hire murderers and buy drugs. You all, people like you."

IN MY SECOND YEAR OF HIGH SCHOOL I dyed my hair black with henna, a temporary and supposedly non-damaging dye that left my scalp stained while locks of my hair fell out like I was in chemo. In school no one said anything about it; they were used to girls going a little crazy, it's what a girl that age does. The history teacher was particularly nice to me, even though I wasn't a good student. One afternoon as we were leaving she asked me if I'd like to meet her daughter. She was shaking, I remember, and smoking: these days if a teacher smokes in front of a student it's vaguely shameful, but twenty years ago it went unnoticed. Before I could answer her, she took out a binder with black covers and showed it to me. It had spiral-bound pages and they were covered with drawings and notes. The drawings were of a woman with black hair and a black dress, and she was sitting among autumn leaves, or graves, or entering a forest. A beautiful and tall witch, drawn in pencil. There was also a drawing of a girl covered in a veil, like for a wedding or an old-fashioned First Communion, who was carrying spiders in her hands. The writing was something between diary entries and poems. I remember one line clearly; it said, *I want you to slice my gums.*

"It's my daughter's," the teacher said. "She doesn't leave the house, and I think you two could be friends."

I remember, I thought, that the girl drew very well. Also that a girl who drew like that wouldn't have any interest in me. At first I didn't answer the teacher. I didn't know what to tell her, and then I muttered that my parents were waiting for me. It wasn't true—I walked home alone. But when I got there, I told my mother. She didn't say anything either, but later on she disappeared into her bedroom to talk on the phone.

The teacher never came back to school. My mother had talked to the principal. The teacher didn't have any children; she didn't have a daughter who drew witches, not alive or dead. She had lied. I found this out only years later. At the time, my mother told me that the teacher had taken a leave of absence to care for her sick daughter. She'd maintained the existence of the ghost daughter. The principal did too. I believed in the locked-in girl for years, and I even tried to reproduce those drawings of forests, graves, and black dresses, which had been drawn by the hand of a lonely adult.

I don't remember that teacher's last name. I know Marco could find her with his hacking skills, but I'd rather forget that sad woman who wanted to take me home with her one day after class, who knows what for.

---

Marco is green less and less; he prefers orange, the idle status. He's connected but distant, the status closest to gray. Gray is silence and death. He hardly writes to me at all. His mother doesn't know, or rather, I lie to her and say we talk as much as ever. My messages to him build up. Sometimes in the morning I find he's replied to them.

When he turns green again one night, he's the first to talk. "How do you know it's me?" he says. He can't see me, so I can cry without shame. These days there are programs, he tells me, that can reproduce someone who has died. They take all the person's information that's disseminated throughout the Internet, and they act according to that script. It's not so different from when they show you personalized ads.

"If you were a machine you wouldn't say this to me."

"No," he writes. "But, how will you know once I *am* a machine?"

"I'm not going to know," I reply. "That program doesn't exist yet; you got that idea from a movie."

"It's a beautiful idea," he writes.

I agree and I wait. Now he has nothing more to say, nothing about red rooms or vengeful ghosts. When he stops talking to me for good I'm going to lie to his mother. I'll invent fabulous conversations; I'll give her hope. *Last night he told me he wants to come out,* I'll tell her while we sip coffee. I hope he decides to run away while she's sleeping her chemical sleep. I hope the food doesn't start to accumulate in the hallway. I hope we don't have to break down the door.

# Things We Lost in the Fire

The subway girl was first. Some people would dispute that, or at least they would deny that she had the power or influence to instigate the bonfires all alone. And all alone she was: the subway girl preached on the city's six underground train lines, and no one was ever with her. But she was unforgettable. Her face and arms had been completely disfigured by deep, extensive burns. She talked to the passengers about how long it had taken her to recover, about the months of infections, hospitals, and pain. Her mouth was lipless and her nose had been sloppily reconstructed. She had only one eye left—the other was a hollow of skin—and her whole face, head, and neck were a maroon mask crisscrossed by spiderwebs. On the nape of her neck she still had one lock of long hair left, which emphasized the masklike effect; it was the only part of her head the fire hadn't touched. Nor had it reached her hands, which were dark and always a little dirty from handling the money she begged for.

Her method was audacious: she got on the train, and if there weren't many passengers, if almost everyone had a seat, she greeted each of them with a kiss on the cheek. Some turned their faces away in disgust, even with a muffled shriek; others accepted the kiss and felt good about themselves; some just let the revulsion raise the hair on their arms, and if she saw this, in summer when people's skin was bare, she'd caress the scared little hairs with her grubby fingers and smile with her mouth that was a slash. Some people even got off the train if they saw her get on. They already knew her routine and wanted to avoid the kiss from that horrible face.

To make matters worse, the subway girl wore tight jeans, see-through blouses, even high-heeled sandals when it was hot out. She wore bracelets on her wrists, and little gold necklaces hung around her neck. For her to flaunt a sensuous body seemed inexplicably offensive.

When she begged for money she was very clear: she wasn't saving up for plastic surgery. There was no use, she would never get her normal face back, and she knew it. She only needed money to cover her expenses, for rent, for food—no one would give her work with a face like that, not even in jobs where the public wouldn't see her. And always, when she finished telling her audience about her days in the hospital, she named the man who had burned her: Juan Martín Pozzi, her husband. She'd been married to him for three years. They had no children. He thought she was cheating on him and he was right—she'd been about to leave him. To keep that from happening, he ruined her. Decided she would belong to no one else. While she was sleeping, he poured alcohol over her face and held a lighter to it. While she couldn't talk, when she was in the hospital and everyone was expecting her to die, Pozzi claimed she'd burned herself, that she'd spilled alcohol during a fight and then tried to smoke a cigarette, still wet.

"And they believed him." The subway girl smiled with her lipless, reptilian mouth. "Even my father believed him."

As soon as she could talk, still recovering in the hospital, she told the truth. Now he was in jail.

When the burned girl left the subway car no one talked about her, but the silence that was left, broken by the shaking as the train moved over the rails, said, *How disgusting, how frightening, I'll never forget her, how can someone live like that?*

*Maybe it wasn't the subway girl who started it all,* thought Silvina, *but she definitely introduced the idea in* my *family.* It had been a Sunday afternoon, and she and her mother were coming back from the movies—a rare excursion, since they almost never went out together. On the train, the subway girl got into their car, gave kisses to the passengers, and told her story. When she finished, she thanked everyone and got off at the next stop. The usual uncomfortable and ashamed silence didn't follow. A boy, who couldn't have been more than twenty years old, started saying, "How manipulative, how gross, how desperate." He also cracked jokes. Silvina remembered how her mother—tall, with short, gray hair, her whole aspect one of authority and power—had walked to the boy, crossing the aisle almost unwaveringly though the train shook as much as always. She'd drawn back her arm and punched the boy in the nose, a decisive and professional blow that made him bleed and cry out, "You old bitch, what's wrong with you?" But her mother didn't respond, not to the boy crying in pain nor to the other passengers, who weren't sure whether to berate her or come to her defense. Silvina remembered the quick look, the silent instruction in her mother's eyes, and how they'd both shot out of the train as soon as the doors opened, how they'd kept running up the stairs from the platform even though Silvina wasn't in good shape and she got tired right away—running made her cough—and her mother was over sixty years old. No one followed them, but they didn't realize it at first. On the busy corner of Corrientes and Pueyrredón they mixed in with the crowd to shake off any guards, or even police, but after two hundred meters they realized they were safe. Silvina couldn't forget her mother's elated laughter, so relieved. It had been years since she'd seen her so happy.

Still, it took Lucila and the epidemic she unleashed for the bonfires to start. Lucila was a model and she was very beautiful, but more than that she had a quirky charm about her. In TV interviews she seemed distracted and guileless, but she had intelligent and audacious things to say, and she became famous for that, too. Or half famous. True celebrity only came when she announced she was dating Mario Ponte, number 7 on the Unidos de Córdoba team. They were a second-division club that had heroically made it to the first, and they'd remained among the best during two championships thanks to a great squad, but above all thanks to Mario, who was an extraordinary player. He had rejected offers from European clubs out of pure loyalty—although some commentators said that at thirty-two and with the level of competition in Europe, it was better for Mario to become a local legend than a transatlantic failure. Lucila seemed to be in love, and though the couple got a lot of media coverage, no one scrutinized them too closely. They were perfect and happy—quite simply, they lacked drama. She got better modeling contracts and closed out all the fashion shows; he bought himself a very expensive car.

Drama came one morning at dawn when they carried Lucila on a stretcher out of her and Mario's apartment: seventy percent of her body was burned, and they said she wouldn't survive. She survived a week.

Silvina vaguely remembered the news reports, the gossip around the office. He had burned her during a fight, they said. Just like with the subway girl, he'd poured a bottle of alcohol over her while she was in bed, and then he'd thrown a lit match onto her naked body. He let her burn a few minutes before covering her with the bedspread. Then he called the ambulance. Like the subway girl's husband, he claimed that she'd done it to herself.

That's why, when women started burning themselves for real, no one believed it at first, Silvina thought while she waited for the bus (she didn't use her own car to visit her mother, since she knew she could be followed). People preferred to believe those women were protecting their men, that they were still afraid of them, in shock and unable to tell the truth. The bonfires were just too hard to comprehend.

Now that there was another bonfire every week, no one knew what to say or how to stop them, except through the usual measures: inspections, police, surveillance. None of it worked. Once, an anorexic friend of Silvina's had told her, "They can't force you to eat."

"Yes, they can," Silvina answered, "they can feed you intravenously, through a tube."

"Yes, but they can't watch you all the time. You cut the tube. You cut off the fluid. No one can watch you twenty-four hours a day. People sleep." It was true. That high school classmate had ended up dying. Silvina sat down with her backpack on her lap. She was glad she didn't have to stand during the ride. She was always afraid a thief would open her backpack and find out what she was carrying.

---

A LOT OF WOMEN WERE BURNED before the bonfires began. It was contagious, explained the experts in domestic violence, in newspapers and magazines and on radio and television, anywhere they could pontificate. It was a complex subject to report on, they said, because on one hand it was necessary to sound the alarm about the femicides, and on the other hand the reports had a ripple effect, similar to what happens among teenagers with suicide. Men were burning their girlfriends, wives, lovers, all over the country. Most of the time they used alcohol, like Ponte (he had already been a hero to so many), but they also used acid, and in one particularly horrible case a woman had been thrown onto a pile of burning tires, part of some worker protest, in the middle of the highway. But Silvina and her mother only mobilized—singly, without consulting one another—after what happened to Lorena Pérez and her daughter, the last murders before the first bonfires. The father, before killing himself, had set fire to mother and daughter with the now tried-and-true bottle of alcohol. They didn't know the victims, but Silvina and her mother both went to the hospital to try to visit them, or to at least protest outside; they ran into each other there. And the subway girl was there too.

But she wasn't alone, not anymore. Now she was accompanied by a group of women of various ages, none of them burned. When the cameras arrived, the subway girl and her companions moved into the spotlight. She told her story, and the others nodded and shouted encouragement. Then the subway girl said something dreadful, brutal:

"If they go on like this, men are going to have to get used to us. Soon most women are going to look like me, if they don't die. And wouldn't that be nice? A new kind of beauty."

Once the cameras had gone, Silvina's mother approached the subway girl and her companions. Several of the women were over sixty years old, and Silvina was surprised to see them so willing to spend the night in the street, to camp out on the sidewalk and paint their signs saying *WE WILL BE BURNED NO MORE.* Silvina stayed with them too, and in the morning she went to the office without having slept. Her coworkers hadn't even heard about the burning of the mother and daughter. They're getting used to it, thought Silvina. The fact that the girl is a child makes the case a little more horrible, but only a little. She spent the morning sending messages to her mother, who didn't answer a single one. She was pretty bad about texting, so Silvina didn't worry. At night, she called her at home and couldn't reach her there either. Was she still at the hospital? Silvina went to look, but the women had abandoned their camp. All that remained were a few scattered markers and some empty snack wrappers swirling in the wind. There was a storm brewing, and Silvina rushed home as fast as she could because she'd left the windows open.

The girl and her mother had died during the night.

SILVINA'S FIRST BONFIRE had taken place in a field off Route 3. The security measures were still very basic then—those of the authorities and of the Burning Women. Many people still refused to believe. True, the case of the woman who'd burned in her own car out in the Patagonian desert had been very strange. The preliminary investigations showed that she'd poured gasoline on the car and then gotten in behind the wheel, and that she'd sparked the lighter herself. No one else: there were no tracks from any other car and it would have been impossible to hide them in the desert, and no one would have been able to get there on foot. A suicide, they said, a very strange suicide. The poor girl must have gotten the idea from all those burned women. We don't know why these attacks are happening in Argentina. These things belong in Arab countries, in India.

"They're some real sons of bitches, Silvinita, dear. Have a seat," said María Helena, her mother's friend and the head of a secret hospital for the burned. She had established it far from the city in the shell of her family's old estate, surrounded by cows and soy. "I don't know why that girl did what she did instead of getting in touch with us, but fine, maybe she wanted to die. That was her right. But these sons of bitches who say that burnings are for Arabs or Indians . . ."

María Helena dried her hands—she'd been peeling peaches for a cake—and looked Silvina in the eye.

"Burnings are the work of men. They have always burned us. Now we are burning ourselves. But we're not going to die; we're going to flaunt our scars."

The cake was in honor of one of the Burning Women, who had survived her first year. Some of those who went to the bonfires chose to recuperate in regular hospitals, but many preferred secret centers like María Helena's. There were others like it, Silvina wasn't sure how many.

"The problem is that they don't believe us. We tell them that we burn ourselves because we want to, but they don't believe us. Of course, we can't make the girls who are staying here talk; we might go to jail."

"We could film a ceremony," said Silvina.

"We thought about that, but it would invade the girl's privacy."

"Right, but what if one of them wanted it to be seen? And we could ask her to go toward the bonfire with, I don't know, a mask, a disguise, if she wants to cover her face."

"What if they can tell where the place is?"

"Oh, María, the pampa all looks the same. If we have the ceremony out in the grasslands, how will they know where it is?"

And, almost without thinking about it, Silvina volunteered to take charge of the filming if one of the girls ever wanted her Burn to go public. María Helena got in touch with her less than a month after she offered. She would be the only one in the ceremony authorized to have electronic equipment. Silvina arrived by car—back then, it was still fairly safe. Route 3 was almost deserted, only a few trucks out on the road. She could listen to music and try not to think: not about her mother, who was in charge of another clandestine hospital in an enormous house in the southern part of Buenos Aires. Her mother, always so fearless and bold, much more so than Silvina, who went on working at the office and still couldn't get up the nerve to join the women. Or about her father, dead since she was a little girl, a good and somewhat inept man. ("Don't ever think I'm doing this because of your father," her mother said to her once, on a break outside the makeshift hospital, while she was inspecting the antibiotics Silvina had brought her. "Your father was a delicious man, he never made me suffer.") Or about her ex-boyfriend, with whom she'd ended things once she realized her mother's radicalization was definitive, because she knew he would inevitably pose a danger to them. Or about whether she should betray the organization herself, tear it apart from within. Since when did people have a right to burn themselves alive? Why did she have to respect these women's wishes?

The ceremony took place at dusk. Silvina used the video

function on a regular camera; phones were forbidden, she didn't have a camcorder, and she didn't want to buy one in case it could be traced. She filmed everything: the women preparing the pyre with enormous dry branches from trees in the countryside, the fire fed with newspapers and gas until the flames stood over a meter high. They were out in the backcountry, and a grove of trees and the house shielded the ceremony from the highway. The other road, to the right, was too far away for anyone to see them. There were no neighbors or workmen. Not at that hour. When the sun set, the chosen woman walked toward the fire. She walked slowly. Silvina thought the girl was going to change her mind because she cried the whole time. She had chosen a song for her ceremony, which the others—around ten, not many—were singing: "Your body, to the fire it goes / consumed quickly, devoured untouched." But she didn't change her mind. The woman entered the fire as if it were a swimming pool; she dove in, ready to sink. There was no doubt she did it of her own will. A superstitious or provoked will, but her own. She burned for barely twenty seconds. Then two women in asbestos suits dragged her out of the flames and carried her at a run to the hospital. Silvina stopped filming before the building came into view.

That night she put the video online. By the next day, millions of people had seen it.

So Silvina took the bus. Her mother was no longer the head of the clandestine hospital on the city's south side. She'd had to move when the secret of the century-old stone house, formerly an old folks' home, had been discovered by one woman's enraged parents ("She has children! She has children!" they'd screamed). Her mother had managed to escape the raid. She'd been tipped off by a neighbor who was a collaborator of the Burning Women, an activist who kept her distance, like Silvina. They had reassigned Silvina's mother to a secret clinic in Belgrano—after an entire year of raids, they'd decided the city was safer than secluded locations. María Helena's hospital had fallen too, though they never discovered the estate had been a location for the bonfires. Out in the country there's nothing more common than burning fields or leaves, so there would always be scorched grass and earth out there.

The judges expedited orders for raids, and in spite of the protests, women who didn't have families or who were simply out alone in public fell under suspicion. The police would make them open their purses, their backpacks, the trunks of their cars, anytime and anywhere. The harassment was getting worse lately, because the bonfires had escalated. In the beginning there'd been one every five months, and now there was a bonfire a week. And those were just the burnings on record, the ones where the women went to a public hospital.

And, just like that high school classmate of Silvina's, the women managed to elude the surveillance remarkably well. The countryside was still vast, and couldn't be monitored by satellite: plus, everyone has a price. If tons of drugs could be smuggled into the country, how were the authorities not going to let the occasional car pass with more drums of gasoline than was strictly reasonable? That was the only thing they needed, because the branches for the bonfires were already there, at every site. And the women brought their desire with them.

"It's not going to stop," the subway girl said in a TV interview. "Look on the bright side," she laughed with her reptile mouth. "At least there's no more prostitution. No one wants a burned monster, or a crazy Argentine woman who could go off one day and set herself on fire—she could burn the customer too."

ONE NIGHT, WHEN SILVINA WAS WAITING for her mother to call about another delivery of antibiotics (she'd have to collect them from the Burning Women collaborators who worked in the city's hospitals), she was struck by a sudden desire to talk with her ex-boyfriend. Her mouth was full of whiskey and her nose of cigarette smoke and the smell of sterilized gauze, the kind used for burns. It was a smell that never left her, along with that of burned human flesh, so difficult to describe. Mostly it smelled of gasoline, only with something more behind it, something unforgettable and strangely warm. But Silvina stopped herself from calling him. She'd seen him on the street with another girl. These days, of course, that didn't mean much. Many women tried not to be alone in public now so the police wouldn't bother them. Everything was different since the bonfires started. Just a few weeks earlier, the first survivors had started to show themselves. To take the bus. Go shopping at the supermarket. To take taxis and subways, open bank accounts, and enjoy a cup of coffee on the terraces of bars, their horrible faces lit by the afternoon sun, their hands—sometimes missing fingers—cupped around mugs. Would they find work? When would the longed-for world of men and monsters come?

Silvina and her mother visited María Helena in jail. At first they'd been afraid that the other inmates would attack her, but no, they treated her remarkably well. "It's because I talk with the girls here. I tell them that we women have always been burned—they burned us for four centuries! The girls can't believe it, they didn't know anything about the witch trials, isn't it incredible? Education in this country has gone to shit. But they're interested, they want to learn."

"What do they want to learn?" asked Silvina.

"Well, they want to know when the bonfires are going to stop."

"And when *are* they going to stop?"

"Oh, what do I know, child. If I had my way they'd never stop!"

The jail's visiting room was a big open hall with many tables, each with three chairs: one for the prisoner, two for visitors. María Helena spoke in a low voice. She didn't trust the guards.

"Some girls say they're going to stop when they reach the number of witches hunted during the Inquisition."

"That's a lot," said Silvina.

"It depends," interrupted her mother. "Some historians say it was hundreds of thousands, others only forty thousand."

"Forty thousand is a lot," murmured Silvina.

"Over four centuries it's not that many," her mother said.

"There weren't many people in Europe six centuries ago, Mom."

Silvina felt the fury fill her eyes with tears. María Helena opened her mouth and said something else but Silvina didn't hear it, and her mother went on and the two women conversed in the sickly light of the prison visitors' room and Silvina heard only how the two of them were too old, they wouldn't survive a Burn, the infection would carry them off in a second. But Silvinita, oh, when Silvina burned it would be beautiful, she'd be a true flower of fire.

## TRANSLATOR'S NOTE

A shadow hangs over Argentina and its literature. Like many of the adolescent democracies of the Southern Cone, the country is haunted by the specter of recent dictatorships, and the memory of violence there is still raw. Argentina's twentieth century was scarred by decades of conflict between leftist guerrillas and state and military forces. The last of many coups took place in 1976, three years after Mariana Enriquez was born, and the military dictatorship it installed lasted until 1983. The dictatorship was a period of brutal repression and state terrorism, and thousands of people were murdered or disappeared. Since the dictatorship fell, Argentina has lived its longest period of democracy in recent history. Generations, including Mariana Enriquez's, have lived their early years under the yoke of dictatorship and come of age in democracy.

In Mariana Enriquez's stories, Argentina's particular history combines with an aesthetic many have tied to the gothic horror tradition of the English-speaking world. She's been compared to Shirley Jackson, and her depictions of a labyrinthine and sinister Buenos Aires echo Victorian gothic renderings of London. Latin

America has a gothic tradition as well, according to the critic María Negroni, that overlaps with what we're used to thinking of as magical realism. Enriquez is the heir, perhaps, of Argentine gothic: Cortázar, Borges, Arlt, and Silvina Ocampo; it's no coincidence that Enriquez wrote a biography of Ocampo, or that the protagonist of this book's title story is named Silvina. But Enriquez's literature conforms to no genre, and gothic is only one corner of the map of her aesthetic.

What there is of gothic horror in the stories in *Things We Lost in the Fire* mingles with and is intensified by their sharp social criticism. Haunted houses and deformed children exist on the same plane as extreme poverty, drugs, and criminal pollution. Her characters occupy an Argentina scarred by the Dirty Wars of the 1970s and '80s; a country whose return to democracy was marked by economic instability, hyperinflation, and precarious infrastructure; a nation that even in this decade has seen egregious instances of femicides and violence against women. Almost all of Enriquez's protagonists, in fact, are women, and in these stories we get a sense of the contingency and danger of occupying a female body, though these women are not victims. The Chilean critic Lorena Amaro emphasizes that most of Mariana's characters exist in a border space between the comfortable *here* and the vulnerable *there*; this latter could be a violent slum or a mysteriously living house, but it operates according to an unknown and sinister rationale, and it is frighteningly near.

In "The Dirty Kid," the narrator is a middle-class woman who chooses to live in the dangerous neighborhood of Constitución. The story has overt violence and hints of the supernatural, but for me one of its most disturbing lines is when the narrator says: "I realized . . . how little I cared about people, how natural these desperate lives seemed to me." The horror comes not only from turning our gaze on desperate populations; it comes from realizing the extent of our blindness.

In "Spiderweb," a suffocating atmosphere of unease comes on the one hand from the looming presence of soldiers serving Alfredo Stroessner, the Paraguayan dictator, and on the other from the images of a lurking, violent natural world: the characters are caught between the brutality of man and that of nature. In "The Inn," the girls' everyday adolescent world of new sexuality and small revenge limns a horrifying history of state terror and clandestine torture centers. Silvina, in the title story, sympathizes with the Burning Women movement but doesn't commit entirely, even toying with the option of destroying it from within. We understand that her choices are to betray her mother and the activists, or to burn herself—she cannot remain in between. The horror comes when Enriquez's characters have to acknowledge their border position, to recognize the other reality and see themselves according to a different and dreadful new logic. As Amaro says, "The fear comes from looking into the courtyard next door and realizing that one day you could be trapped there, in a world that seems near, but is unknown and terrifying."

This is Enriquez's first book translated to English, but she has a long publication history; much of her previous short story work has also employed the tools of horror, though often in more intimate or personal settings. *Things We Lost in the Fire* is her work that most employs the tools of realism, and also the one that most mines Argentine culture and history for its horror. As Enriquez has said herself, the stories here have something of the supernatural to them, but the fear comes more from police, neighborhoods, poverty, violence, and men. "The Intoxicated Years," for example, delves into the period of *alfonsinísmo*.

Raúl Alfonsín was democratically elected when the dicatorship ended in 1983; the period of his government, though, had its own kind of terror. People were depressed and isolated, literally in the dark, the atmosphere charged with anxiety. There are few to no supernatural elements in the story, but the horror is there—a horror specific to being an adolescent in a particular political moment, but also a more animal fear that comes from living in a world that has seemingly forgotten you.

Mariana Enriquez's particular genius catches us off guard by how quickly we can slip from the familiar into a new and unknown horror. The wraiths of Argentina's violent past appear in her stories, but ultimately Enriquez's literature is not tied to any time or place. Rather, it appeals to ancient, creeping fears that prowl our subconscious, and that, in the worst of times, are acted out on our political stage.

## ABOUT THE AUTHOR

MARIANA ENRIQUEZ is a writer and editor based in Buenos Aires, where she contributes both fiction and nonfiction to a number of newspapers and literary journals.